SCATTERED
LOVE

'I bury my head in books as the ostrich does in the sand.'
–William Butler Yeats

SCATTERED LOVE

LES AMOURS DISPERSÉES

MAYLIS BESSERIE

TRANSLATED BY CLÍONA NÍ RÍORDÁIN

THE LILLIPUT PRESS
DUBLIN

To her, somewhere among the clouds above.

First published in English in 2023 by
THE LILLIPUT PRESS
62–63 Sitric Road, Arbour Hill
Dublin 7, Ireland
www.lilliputpress.ie

First edition, *Les amours disperses* © Editions GALLIMARD, Paris, 2023

Paperback ISBN 9781843518624

10 9 8 7 6 5 4 3 2 1

The Lilliput Press gratefully acknowledges the financial
support of the Arts Council/An Chomhairle Ealaíon.

Set in 10.25pt on 16.5pt Le Monde Livre by iota (www.iota-books.ie)
Printed in Poland by Drukarnia Skleniarz

I

The coffin is so small it might be a child's coffin. As if the old woman had lived her life in the round, as if she had come back to the beginning. Madeleine wonders if her neighbour finds the coffin too narrow, wonders if the sateen pillow was plumped up by the people in the funeral home before they laid her head on it and if she is lying comfortably there under the lid. Four men in matching suits lift the casket and hoist it easily onto their shoulders. Over the years her neighbour had become lighter and lighter, and when she died, well into her nineties, she was as lithe as a liana. She lived life to the full and died peacefully in her sleep. 'The kind of death you wish for,' Madeleine says to herself as she walks with the neighbour's family behind the coffin, accompanying her to her final home. She slipped away without any pain or suffering in the early morning, which was when she usually woke up: it was a kind of false start; her eyes opened and they closed again

1

just as quickly – and that was it. Madeleine would like to go in the same way, bowing out of the world without a whimper, but something tells her that it won't happen like that. She imagines the pain in her left arm, the neck-breaking fall on the hard edges of the stairs, a weight like an elephant's foot pressing down on her chest and her phone out of reach. She could put up with such an end as long as it was swift and she didn't linger. She has already prepared for such an eventuality, already filled out the papers that never leave her wallet.

If my mental functions become permanently impaired with no likelihood of improvement, if the impairment is so severe that I do not understand what is happening to me and my physical condition means that medical treatment would be needed to keep me alive: I do not wish to be kept alive by such means. I wish medical treatment to be limited to keeping me comfortable and free from pain, and I refuse all other medical treatment.

For the funeral, she's not sure yet. The family vault is choc-a-bloc, so if she wants to join her loved ones she will have to make herself very small – fit into an urn after being consumed by the flames. She dreads the ordeal, thinks about it sometimes and then puts it off, saying to herself, 'There's time enough yet.'

Her elderly neighbour had decided on the question of the last resting place without dallying – no frills, a standard ceremony, a funeral mass in Saint Joseph's church and burial in the old cemetery of Saint-Pancrace. She departed this life in the middle of summer, her wooden coffin shining in the sunlight. She has gone to lie under the cool stone, feet towards the water, facing the mirror-like sea that saw her live out her life and grow old. An accomplished death. The old lady had been ready for several years, waiting to move on with patience, curiosity and the delectation of the believer who is waiting for paradise. Madeleine hopes that the result, whatever it is, lives up to the expectations of her beloved neighbour, who reminded Madeleine of her own grandmother. There was something in her accent, in the way she broke up the syllables as if she were biting them, adding unexpected 'e's and decorating them with the remains of her patois.

They reach the family vault, which welcomes them with open arms, its wide stone mouth already gaping. The old lady's spot is on the third row, above her parents, atop the coffin of her mother, who agrees to carry her on her womb again, as if the century that had taken her away had been a mere parenthesis closed by eternity. The old woman lies next to her dead husband in the marble wedding bed, waiting for their children to come and join them one day, to complete the wooden pyramid, the strange tree formed by the stacked boxes, with the bodies of those who are no longer alive. When Madeleine comes closer to throw down her rose, she notices that the deep cavity is incredibly well organized. She had forgotten how crowded the underground city of graves is – a self-contained world, which will hold every one of them in the end.

They all march wordlessly in single file, each throwing down a rose that bounces and is lost in earth as dark as their formal wear. Madeleine adjusts the silk scarf that flows over her dress with its mother-of-pearl buttons. Her neighbour hated jeans, and, remembering she had once said that dressing properly for a funeral was the final mark of respect due to the dead, Madeleine had left hers aside. Madeleine had honoured her wishes. *Thy will was done. Amen, dear friend.*

During the wake Madeleine allowed herself to be served seconds; she drowned her shyness in the wine from the buffet and the cheese tarts; she endured the others' sadness, their red-rimmed eyes. She stayed for a long time, taking the opportunity to escape her usual solitary evenings. She returned home quite tipsy. It seems to her now that a trumpet is blowing a hail of crochets in her sleep, a deluge of notes that chime with each intake of breath and nip at her heart, carrying her off into the last moments of the night. The trumpet tune makes her mind wander, soar into the heights. Then slowly it fades away. Becomes a whisper. Yields to a completely different sound.

[Radio]

Good morning, everyone, welcome. It's seven o'clock on Tuesday, 21 July 2015, and these are today's headlines …

Madeleine is so familiar with the voice – the way it emphasizes the first syllables and speeds up at the end of sentences, the way it laughs and clears its throat – she is so familiar with it that she does not wake up. She allows the warm, comforting voice of the merman to caress her; he is her bodiless lover who comes to sing under her window every day. The noise he makes soothes her back into a dozy state. Another old woman – not her neighbour but Jeanne, her own grandmother – valiantly uses her arms to pull herself out of her coffin, puts one leg and then the other over the side and hops out. She has come back from the dead, and she raises her arms in a victorious fashion; her grandmother looks at her and cheerfully announces that she has been reincarnated. 'Really?' 'You can see for yourself.' *She is younger than when she died,* Madeleine says to herself, *barely eighty years old,* and her grandmother does seem completely rejuvenated, even playful; she gambols around like a mountain goat, dressed in an old-style peasant dress and a brightly coloured hooded cape, under which her white legs jiggle. She hops around on tiptoe in her boots, with a basket in her hand, like a silver-haired Little Red Riding Hood, her wrinkled cheeks flushed pink as she walks. The path she is walking along winds down a verdant mountain covered in greenery. Her grandmother picks four-leaf clovers for good luck, to keep misfortune at bay.

Madeleine knows what she is about. Neither she nor her grandmother has been spared. Their loved ones fell like flies, in the prime of their lives, as if they were not meant for this world. Madeleine's mother didn't escape the curse; she passed away shortly after Madeleine's birth and joined the crowd of uncles, aunts and young people in the family vault. Was it because they were short of four-leaf clovers or rabbit's feet? All Madeleine knows is that they died, one after the other, before she had time to get to know them. Only her grandmother, the invincible Jeanne, lived on, taking on all the roles, stepping into the shoes of all those who had disappeared, watching over Madeleine until she left the nest. And even beyond. The curse hung over both of them, like a raven with its talons outstretched, ready to land on them at any time. Although they have been spared for the moment – her grandmother lived until she was nearly a hundred, and she herself is unharmed thus far – the curse has nevertheless managed to cast a shadow over their lives, covering them with a veil that sways in the breeze but always returns to its place. The question, 'Granny, would you like a four-leaf clover?', to provide her with an extra dose of good luck, is easily understood. In the dream, Madeleine gives her granny bunches of clover with long stems wrapped around her arthritic fingers, leaving the leaves sticking out above them like rings. Madeleine thanks her, tries to kiss her grandmother and grabs her arm. It is motionless and so thin that the bones protrude under her skin. Her grandmother doesn't react or even look at her anymore; her bright eyes are staring blankly, mirroring the green of the surrounding countryside. When Madeleine's lips reach her granny's hollow cheek, the deathly cold of her cheekbone transfixes her, and all of a sudden she wakes up.

[Radio]

We end this edition with an astonishing story of a mystery at Roquebrune.

 Sixty-seven years ago, the body of the Nobel Prizewinning poet William Butler Yeats was brought home to be buried in Sligo, Ireland. Well, it appears that his body never left France. At least if documents discovered by Daniel Paris, a diplomat's son, are to be believed. In 1939, Yeats's body was buried in the old cemetery at Roquebrune-Cap-Martin while waiting to be transported back to his native country. However, with the outbreak of the Second World War the journey was out of the question. Finally, in 1948, Ireland asked for the poet's body to be returned. The problem was that the body had been thrown into a mass grave, making it impossible to identify his remains among the bones of all the other people interred in the grave. The documents found today bear witness to a major diplomatic incident. Who is buried in Drumcliff Cemetery, in the grave visited each year by poetry fans from all over the world? Has Yeats remained at Roquebrune in Saint-Pancrace's seaside cemetery? For the moment, it would appear that no investigation has been launched ...

Imagine that. A mystery in the old cemetery where Madeleine was yesterday. Her neighbour is still on her mind. Was it a shaggy-dog story or a supernatural event? Why did the radio voice mention the name of her town? Such a rare event. Did a light emerge from the usually cloudless Provençal sky or, perhaps, from the damp seashore? As she stirs her hot black coffee, Madeleine imagines herself in the fog that precedes the arrival of the ghost; she can already hear the hissing of the rattlesnake in the night, the cawing of the crow and the squealing of the rat. From her vantage point, she can see the darkness dissipate to reveal the glistening face of a hardy ghost, dripping with mud, daubed with the ashes of hell. 'Ah ha!' She can imagine everything about the Irish poet she has never heard of. Were his final wishes flouted? Is he coming back to earth, after decades in purgatory, to exact his revenge and wreak havoc in the little town on the French Riviera? 'Hmm.' Unless the so-called ghost simply wants to tread the rocky ground again with his fleet feet? After all, what do we know about ghostly pleasures, about what goes on behind the sheets? The steam is whisked away by her spoon, and her coffee now looks like the swirling black dress of a widow. Madeleine downs it in one go. This graveyard story intrigues her; she starts browsing on her phone for articles, digging deep in the obscure parts of the web for traces of this celebrated secret, wondering what spider could have tied the poet up with its thread for so long. Her fingers probe the screen frantically, as if they were digging directly into the soil of Roquebrune – six feet under, to be precise. The headlines from the wire services gush out and bounce back as if from the depths of the device, all asking the same question about the death of the great poet, about the identity of the person whose remains lie in his coffin. Not a word for the others, the nameless dead, the unknown bones in the grave. Hapless afterthoughts. Unclaimed handfuls of stardust. Madeleine's good humour is gone, driven away suddenly by a gust of anger that contorts her mouth and furrows her brow. She is incensed by what she's reading: the mass grave was opened, and they went through the motions of choosing the remains; they helped themselves. To what purpose? To fill the coffin of a poet and send him back to Ireland? Madeleine sees men in suits giving orders in front of the open maw of the grave. She scrunches up her eyes to block out the macabre visions that have suddenly appeared at her table – a gaping hole, torn flesh, tattered clothes, scattered bones. Like many inhabitants of Roquebrune, Madeleine also has a deceased relative in the grave, a stillborn ancestor, a skeleton in the cupboard – whom she often thinks of without really knowing why; the story slipped between the slats, into the pits of family memory. What happened to that body, to those remains and to the remains of the others scattered in the common grave? Are those ordinary souls of no interest to anyone? Have their bodies been desecrated to serve as under-studies in the poet's coffin? Madeleine feels that her rage is opening a deep wound that has been passed on to her like a birthmark. The ragged stitches of the wound give way, one by one, as her body swells with disgust and rage. Yes, she wants to know the answer. Her whole being wants to know what happened. What happened to her relative's dead body, and to all the other dead bodies in the pit? She refuses to accept that they have been buried and forgotten once again. She will not be alone in defending their rights. She will bring together all the living descendants of these post-mortem victims if necessary. All those who are collateral damage.

William

The prophecy is still there, hanging in the clouds, the prophecy of the enchantress who guided my verses. Who drew up my chart. Blavatsky's prophecy hovers above me, six feet above my cloud, her voice whirling. Her voice is like a stream that lifts the stones. The invisible masters lend their words to the enchantress. They speak through her, our ancestors, our forefathers. They all tell the same story. The story of Maud Gonne, the woman who guided my dreams, who bound me tight in her nets, who still holds me captive on my cloud. It's not over yet. I drink the words of the woman who sees. They take me back to my beloved, my love has not disappeared, it still vibrates in the voice of the oracle. *Maud has not gone.*

'*Drink your coffee, William, and don't forget to leave some grounds at the bottom. Once you finish it, I'll turn the cup upside down, tip it onto the saucer as if it were a lid and let the universe reveal itself. Sometimes it sticks to the saucer, they say* it's the "prophet's coffee cup" and there's no need to separate them. You know all your wishes will come true. Are you ready? Look, the black slime has dissipated. Everything is there before you. All you have to do is read it.

'You are going to be like an eagle with its hands twisted, standing with its beak. On this eagle, there is a "V". On the front of its beak. Do you see it, William? If you see it, it means you are a seer, only seers and painters see. It's the "V" of victory. You will emerge from this trial and come out triumphant, like him, like the eagle. Look at the bird, you can see its chest. Someone is hiding under its chest. See that figure sticking its head under the bird's neck? That is you. You are sheltered by the bird, a noble bird, an eagle.

'Next to you, a knot is being untied. Can you see the white knot? Something in your life has suddenly become undone. It is still unravelling. Look closely at the cup, there is an unravelled ribbon. It is wrinkled. There is one last knot. A tiny one. It must be untied, William. Without question.

'Follow the powder, against the knot, I see a tooth. A tooth that was pulled. That was hurting you. The tooth was pulled out, the pain is gone. A very old pain. The burden of your ances-tors, tied up in your jaw. It was a prisoner in your mouth. Sing the song of your ancestors, William. It must come out.

'Look, it's a bird, a golden bird – the coffee grounds are lighter, can you see? It's a bird with a long tail. Like a blackbird or a crane. This is good news. A good omen. The omen is near. It is at hand. It is there, under your house.

'Look closely at that spot in the cup and see the long woman with curls that curl around her face. The woman is standing. You can see her completely clearly, that's rare – you can see she is determined, ready to listen to the secrets of the stones. The stones know. They crack open to let in the man who whispers; he is invisible. He is you, William. You are the shade of that woman in the stone. A shade that visits her, that surrounds her like a fog. You are all around her. Invisible but palpable. Look at the coffee grounds in the cup, you are hidden behind those stones. Stuck in the rock. Without her, without that woman, you can't get out. Without the standing woman, nothing is possible. You are bound together like the souls of the dead. Look at the white path that goes from you to her on the cup. It is a cycle: she breathes your dreams into you, and you spread them under her feet. You must listen to her. Allow your dreams to flow on her back, become the boat that carries souls down the river, float and let the waves carry you to the top of the cup.

'At the top, a big fish is waiting for you, William. Waiting for her too. A beautiful fish, a big one. It looks like a salmon. Can you see it? Can you see its eye? The fish is money. For you, it's a treasure. A treasure waiting at the bottom of the cup. Hidden in the crashing waves. In the ebb and flow.

'And what you see there, the triangle is a winged triangle on the tail of the fish. A winged triangle, which will show you how the wind is blowing. It will guide you on your journey. It will lead you to your destiny. To this fish. Look, it's huge. It has spots. I don't know what it is. A huge fish. Maybe a pike? William, this treasure is for you.

'Now, look at the bottom of the cup. You must learn to read it, William. Follow the line, along the wall. Don't let go. Let your eyes glide over the porcelain. It leads you to the seahorse that is hidden under the powder. A toothed seahorse. You'll land on its back. A stroke of luck, a charm. And next to the seahorse, *a white surface, do you see it? A white surface with small rocks sticking out – one, two, three, you have to jump on them to get across. This means that the path is opening. Take small steps and it will open up. Every week you will get new information, and every week you will learn something different. The road is opening up little by little. Bit by bit. Take little leaps, little leaps, and you will reach the cove, you will settle down like the bird sitting in its nest. Look how well the bird perches on the cup. You'll be like him, William.*

'Remember, you are the man protected by the rock. But before you can reach the fish, before you can be like the bird, there are the rocks. And in the background? I can see a lion. A lion at the bottom of your cup, William. A lion with a man's head. A head that turns around to look at the past.

2

SOUTHERN ENTRANCE TO SAINT-PANCRACE CEMETERY
ROQUEBRUNE-CAP-MARTIN
2708–2846 PROMENADE DE LA 1ère DIVISION FRANÇAISE LIBRE
OPENING TIME: 8.30 AM
CLOSING TIME: 5 PM
TEL. CARETAKER: 06.53.85.48.76

At this hour of the day, the cemetery is open; the camera is on; the chain is coiled around the foot of the gate like a snake. The sky diffuses the soft colours of the setting sun; the evening breeze is strong, blowing the sixty-year-old's hardy frame towards the entrance. He left his cobbler's shop early to arrive ahead of the others and parked in front of the cemetery. Now he is opening the boot, unloading the table and chairs and taking out the documents for the meeting. He has organized everything – told the caretaker about their initiative, explained why half a dozen men and women would be arriving at the old cemetery to wander among their silent ancestors, where the crosses and the graves will stare back at them. The good-humoured caretaker with the twinkly eyes had no objections. He saw no problem in allowing the group into the place of rest over which he keeps watch, as long as they showed respect for their dusty neighbours, the residents of the floor below.

Everything goes according to plan. It all starts where it all began – in the cemetery. Set on a hillside high above the old town, it slopes down unimpeded to meet the sea that lies in front of it. The cobbler follows the winding vertical path that heads straight for the shore. He glides down the endless grey stone steps, holding tightly to the black handrail that splits the cemetery in two, creating a border between the terraces, where the oldest graves in the city lie, and the rest of the tombs. He contemplates the spectacle of the strange, ongoing marriage of beauty and death – the grace of the trees that line the water, their tops colliding with the flinty stones. He walks through the alleys, his grey hair buffeted by the wind, until his legs tire, forcing him to stop for a moment. The grave made of concrete at his feet is strange – it makes him think of an iceberg, an island half-sunken into the ground. At its centre is a cube-shaped stele, like the head of a body whose legs are imprisoned in the ground. Poking out of the darkness, the tomb displays brightly coloured inscriptions, which it flings at the sky of Provence:

HERE LIES CHARLES ÉDOUARD JEANNERET
KNOWN AS LE CORBUSIER

Small stones have been placed on the grave by visitors, admirers of the architect who was swept away by the waves to die in the arms of the Mediterranean Sea. He had lovingly designed the grave himself, ahead of the day when he and his wife would be no more, when their dwelling place would become narrower and darker, when space would no longer matter. His heart gave out, ruptured as he dove into the sea, in that heady jump that precedes a swim. His body sank to the bottom before rising again above the sea, on the mountain that carries the graves on its back like a camel carries its humps. The cobbler is not entirely convinced by the aesthetics of the monument. It stands out from the others, especially the walls that house the funeral recesses – those vertical tombs, superimposed on each other through lack of space, their engraved plaques lined up vertically like so many solicitors' offices. He resumes his walk; feels, through his rubber soles, the gravel that covers the dry earth; mulls over the names he deciphers along the way: painters, decorated Resistance fighters, poets and Russian duchesses – all the great and the good covered by the soil of Saint-Pancrace.

In the distance he can see the shadows of others arriving, people who like himself have responded to Madeleine's invitation on social media; they join him, sitting around the table on the folding chairs he has just set up. As he arrives, one of them, the youngest – a beanpole of a man with a waxy complexion and tattoos showing under his T-shirt

– congratulates him on the little spot he has found at the back of the cemetery, under the tall pine trees. Their small talk – 'You can't say the neighbours are noisy' – does not reflect the emotion they feel today. The cemetery, where the first grave was dug nearly two centuries ago, has been marked by too many wars; saturated with memories and silence, it crushes them with its loftiness, with the splendour of its stones, with nature and the sea that surrounds it. They all know what brings them together today: weighed down by painful family history, they all fear that one of their relatives – a grandfather, an aunt or a cousin – may have been sent to Ireland to be buried instead of the poet. They are all determined to retrieve their dead.

Each has started the investigation by themselves, asking those around them, questioning their immediate families, sharing what they found with the group. Today, on the advice of a lawyer, the group is going to set up an association. Their aim is to build a case, by gathering evidence, so as to start proceedings and obtain the analysis of the remains transported to Ireland. They will demand the truth.

Madeleine has filleted the documents published by the press, the letters from embassies, the reports that miraculously appeared out of the safe. She has written to Daniel Paris, the man who discovered them. He has kindly agreed to meet her in Paris next week.

On this day, 18 September 2015, in the old cemetery of Saint-Pancrace, the association of 'The Scattered' gains legal status. And as this is happening, a bird, probably a peregrine falcon, flaps its speckled wings in the particle-laden air.

The bird flies over the wall and lands on the stele erected in memory of the poet's brief sojourn in the cemetery. Its talons cover a winged unicorn, caught in mid-air, under which is written, 'William Butler Yeats 1865–1939'. The falcon scratches the unicorn with its beak, trying to interrupt its mad dash through the air, and pecks at the stone, trying to crack it.

William

When the face of the moon is hidden, my mind returns to her. No one has been able to chase away the freedom fighter, my own Diana, who drove me from the heavenly world to the lowest circles of hell. She is my little Scotland. My dear Maud. The bee that fed me, the wasp that stung me.

My ears have thoughts only for her. They can hear the voice that makes my cloud tremble. My ears can see the roses raining down on me, burning me like flames. Dear Mr Yeats, she said at the start, back in the age of romanticism. Maud was as old as Christ on the cross, ready to sacrifice herself for Ireland. She was an indomitable warrior. Dear Mr Yeats, my dear friend, she said afterwards, when the future had come to an end. Because of her, I wished for the end of the world so that my despair might cease. The despair of love, of unrequited love. I threw my verses into this paralysing love. Spurned by Maud, I was led to the folds of suffering in which poetry grows. Maud, the Goddess of Tartarus and the Elysian Fields, made me aware of my heart. It yielded to her, not one inch of the surrounding pink and red flesh resisted. Maud squeezed my tried and tested heart so tightly, squeezed it so tight that pink and red verses flowed. My verses. My blood.

3

Madeleine is happy to be travelling to Paris to meet the man who opened his safe of secrets and is now opening his grand Parisian flat to her. To get to Paris, she had to overcome dizzying obstacles – apply for leave on the agency's incomprehensible software, let the new director know. As an estate agent, she is in charge of 'character' residences, a job that gives her the opportunity to travel the country, exploring the bay beyond Roquebrune and Cap Martin, going back and forth to Monaco. She likes to be outdoors most of all, walking around the villas, looking at the trees in the gardens and the old terraced estates known here as *restanques*. In her guise as an estate agent, she likes to go behind the scenes, soaking up the atmosphere, imagining the events that the walls may have witnessed and measuring the joys and sorrows that their cracks conceal. However, for some time now – perhaps since she turned fifty, the weight of her own cracks, her divorce and the new solitude that has come with it – that enjoyment has been dulled. The trip to Paris has come at the right time, offering a breath of fresh air, an unexpected escape. Her commitment to the cause of the dead and abandoned has given her renewed energy tinged with anger, and the enthusiasm of someone who is struggling to solve the enigma of the Sphinx, to get to the truth. She wants to live up to her mission, to the esteem in which she is held by the Scattered, her new acolytes. For her meeting with Daniel Paris, the man who alerted the world to the scandal, she has put on her best suit, high-heeled shoes with ankle-straps that wind around her ankles several times, and a long coat to hide the oversized derrière that makes her feel self-conscious. With her file under her arm, she clatters out of the metro and arrives in front of the freshly cleaned, cream-coloured facade of the building, with winding black balconies, and lion heads framing the windows. In the hall, the marbled floor echoes, the mouldings climb up to the ceiling and draw graceful spirals on the walls. Madeleine passes through a varnished door with a golden handle – so clean that its glass is invisible to the naked eye – and finds herself at the foot of an imposing staircase with a proudly worn red carpet. She assesses the five-storey climb – around a hundred and twenty-five steps – then dejectedly plunges into the tiny metal lift, which is silent as a tomb. It brings her to a midnight-blue door. She rings the bell. No answer. She rings again. There is the sound of footsteps inside. The door finally opens.

*

Hello, my apologies, I didn't hear you. Do take a seat.

Last night, I wrote to the moderator of the Free French veterans' website, to ask him to correct an error about my father – there are always errors about my father, people get mixed up between him and his namesake: a certain Jacques-Émile Paris. So, to be sure, is it my father, *Jacques-Camille Paris*, who interests you?

It has to be said that all these coincidences are incredible – Jacques-Camille and Jacques-Émile Paris both joined General de Gaulle in London during the war; they were both diplomats, and the writer Romain Gary was under their command at different times. It's enough to make your head spin, wouldn't you agree? They even got married on the same day, in Brussels, can you imagine? My mother accidentally received the gifts intended for the other Mrs Paris. That's very odd, isn't it? Have you heard of Romain Gary? I have one of his novels here, *Le Grand vestiaire*. He dedicated it to my father at the time. You see, that's his handwriting: *To Mr Jacques-Camille Paris, with my gratitude, for supporting this book*.

To come back to this story of the two Parises, the homonymy has been a source of errors that are both annoying and embarrassing. The author of a biography devoted to Romain Gary even attributed Jacques-Émile's antics to my father – and, best of all, his affair with a Bulgarian spy. You can imagine the fallout from that – my father, Paul Claudel's son-in-law, carrying on with a Bulgarian spy! Fortunately, the error was rectified.

Yes, indeed, the writer Paul Claudel was my grandfather and Camille Claudel my great-aunt. To tell you the truth, it was while I was going through a trunk at Claudel's castle in Brangues, where my mother lived after my father's death, that I came across his papers relating to Yeats's burial. Let me explain – on his return from London, my father became the director of the European Department at the French Foreign Ministry on the Quai d'Orsay. He was in charge, so to speak, in 1948, when the Irish government asked for the remains of the poet William Butler Yeats to be returned to his native land.

No, I knew very little about Yeats, nor was I familiar with his work. To tell you the truth, I even tended to confuse him with Keats, the English poet – although their names don't quite rhyme. I just knew that Yeats was an important figure, a well-known poet. That's why I was worried about keeping the documents that mentioned him. So I contacted the Irish embassy, which in turn contacted the French foreign ministry. Because my father had received the documents while on duty, the French had to authenticate and approve them before they could be passed on to the Irish – I did not realize that. You see, as far as I was concerned it was Yeats's business, and I felt I had to deal directly with the Irish authorities. Of course, the embassy had the right idea and they took care of things. As for the rest, I don't know what else to tell you.

Yes, of course, I read them at the time, in 2015. I don't remember many of the details, except that I was surprised that a man like Yeats had been thrown into a mass grave. Mind you, it reminds me of what befell my great-aunt. What I mean is that Yeats was not a *poète maudit*, he was an accomplished and respected writer, a Nobel Prizewinner. I was very surprised, as I'm sure my father was, when he heard the story. I also remember that when I read the letters I could see there was great embarrassment, both on the Irish side and on the French side, for the matter. I think they were all very upset about it. You can imagine – after all, Yeats was very well known when he died, so nobody must have been happy with the mess.

That's all I can tell you, Madame. I'm sorry I can't be of more help. It was nice to meet you. Do let me know how your investigation goes.

You're welcome. Good luck.

William

My dear Maud, my life's torment, you appeared on 30 January 1889, a blessed day, a cursed day, in your cabriolet drawn by a mighty, black-hoofed horse. You flew, my crow, over the mean cobbles of London, shaken in your leather cage, from Belgravia to Bedford Park. 'Stop, driver, their home is here.' Your terrible beauty followed you, proud rose of twenty-two, rose of all my days, to our home. I saw the goddess walk, the mother of the fairy people, the Great Queen. I saw her walk past the brick wall and caress the sunflowers. I felt the perfume of her Ireland carry my soul beyond the horizon, beyond the sea, pouring it into the lakes and rivers of the *Sidh*, on the shores of the marvellous islands racked by desolate winds. I was a poet's apprentice, hidden in the shade of my father, hidden in the shade of the painter, John, whose azure canvases bedecked with satyrs covered my youthful dreams. When the august, six-foot-tall figure, the sovereign queen with bronze curls, knocked, I opened.

She entered the house like a shadow. She glided in and glued herself into my eye, between my eyelids, which the dust had shut. Like water in the wood, Maud slipped inside. She was like a divine elixir: one drop for each of my thoughts. She strode into the house, like a majestic lioness, her face split by the cold London light. Maud came with her hands full – with oaths of war against the crown, with oaths for Ireland. She stung my father with her warlike words, touched him to the core. He could already see the fighting, the bullets from the rifles, the bites from the fangs of boars coming out of the mouths of poisonous asps. He imagined the thirsty mouths, the bodies drained of blood, falling asleep, swollen with death. I had Queen Maeve herself before my eyes, her wrists encircled with gold and precious stones, ready to start the battle with her piercing cry, ready to clamour for war and ready to listen, atop her chariot, to the distant clashing of swords and axes. I could feel the breath of the warrior, the Queen of Ireland, and it intoxicated me with the wind of hope, like noble wine.

4

The wind rustles in the old graveyard, moving the folding table on which Madeleine lays the copy of the letter written in blue ink that she is about to read to the others: the first of the letters to be published by *The Irish Times* and all the Irish newspapers anxious to expose the scandalous treatment of Yeats's body. The ambassador's handwriting is as sloppy as that of a quack writing a hurried prescription to get rid of a patient – there are dots missing on the 'i's, trailing crosses on the 't's. Madeleine warns the six members of the association seated in front of her of the difficulty in deciphering certain passages: the faded ink, the illegibility of certain names. Despite this, she starts to read and becomes the voice of the author – Stanislas Ostrorog, French ambassador to Dublin in 1948. He draws the ministry's attention to the thorny question of the transfer of Yeats's remains, a matter which, *if not addressed, could cause serious problems*. He writes a paragraph on the glory of *the greatest contemporary poet in the English language*, outlining the repercussions for France on the diplomatic front, the risks involved. Yeats was a national treasure, the Victor Hugo of Ireland, a Nobel Prizewinner and a senator. So the ambassador fears the mishaps, the fallout if the press ever gets wind of the mess, if people learn of the lies told about his remains.

Before the transfer, he was contacted by Yeats's son Michael, who had just learned that his father was not in his tomb in Roquebrune but in the mass grave. The family knew nothing of the decision. 'Unbelievable!' Madeleine stresses that the action had been taken without their consent. The more of the letter she reads, the more unclear it becomes, floundering in a puddle of arguments that blur the lines and make the reader lose sight of what really happened. Anxious to protect his own interests, the diplomat does not explain Yeats's presence in the mass grave; he blames the family, accusing them of negligence, of not having provided a burial place for their august relative. Paris was worried that the French authorities would be held responsible for the incident, and he hoped to keep it out of the press until the transfer to Ireland and the state funeral had righted the wrong. To cover up the affair, he took all necessary precautions, sent one of his men to Roquebrune to find the body, to put it in a coffin without anyone knowing about it.

Madeleine wonders how Paris's man could have found Yeats in a centuries-old grave among dozens of corpses. She suspects that the ambassador wanted to hide the deception and show that his administration had behaved in a manner above reproach – he had even commissioned a report from his subordinate to that effect. Madeleine and the others speculate about the background to the affair, about the negotiations conducted on the spot between the Quai d'Orsay's man and the Roquebrune authorities, the officials and the undertakers. None of this appears in the letter, but they read between the lines. What is unwritten does not need to be erased. It is the deliberately blank spaces that harbour the scandal within, the pain of the families, the mystery of the fate of the forgotten dead that the Scattered are determined to resolve. Terrifying images of corpses, piled-up remains, limbs entwined in the rigidity of death, now flash around the table in the minds of the descendants who are ready to defend them.

Each one gathered here can feel the dead person they represent resurface in the old cemetery. The cobbler is reminded of the grandfather he knew only through his portrait. The black-and-white photo of him with his incredible handlebar moustache and sideburns sat on his grandmother's bedside table; a dark shadow furrowed her wrinkled face whenever she looked at it, and an awkward silence followed. *A dead silence,* the cobbler used to think when his grandmother's eyes stared piercingly at the picture as if she were seeing through it, before losing herself in the void, as if she had fallen into a well of sorrow. Not a dead man, though, but a ghost who always followed her and made the old woman blush with shame; it had persecuted her to the end. She understood that the ghost was taking a form of justifiable revenge and believed she deserved the painful visions that made her feel guilty. She had failed to save him, failed to free him from the hell into which he had sunk, failed to erase the debts and bitterness that had made him go under. She hadn't even managed to take his body down, hadn't managed to unhook her poor husband whose body was still twitching when she came across it, performing his last dance without her. She had endlessly replayed the scene until she joined him, three decades later. The cobbler could still hear her telling him about the men who had run like the blazes to get there – neighbours who had come to help the doctor, the smell of death in the room. The doctor had dictated the procedure to follow: the knot had to be loosened, the pulse checked and resuscitation started. She stood there, frozen in pain in front of her man – *anoxia, cerebral oedema* – her eyes fixed on the eyes of one who no longer blinked, who could no longer see her, whose eyelids were being closed – *he was pronounced dead at 5.12 pm*. There was nothing left apart from a letter displayed in plain sight, in which he had not known what to say. A few words of apology and then silence. She too had remained silent; she should have prayed, just in case, while he could still hear her. There had been no ceremony, no mass for the hanged man; his parents had disowned their son who had died in a state of sin and had even banished him from the family vault. She had not been able to afford a funeral and had seen him off coffin-less, in a sheet, 'thrown into the grave like a bundle of dirty laundry, like a pauper'. That evening, she had found herself lying at her child's feet so that he would fall asleep. The ghost had come – for the first visit, and he had never left her. Where is he today, the hanged man who was his grand-father? Scattered? His head to the north, his feet to the south? Is there anything left of him nearby, in the cemetery? Has

31

the soil of Roquebrune cemetery finally reconciled them in a nil–all draw? The cobbler would like to know.

As he tries to make sense of it, Madeleine returns to the issue of the identification of the mortal remains sent back to Ireland. How could they have reconstructed Yeats's body with any certainty? Did they take bones at random, any bones that came to hand? A skull here, a tibia there? Did the pieces of the dead cohabiting together in the box form a single creature made up of dozens of bodies? Could the bones of the poet be entirely absent? As long as there was no DNA analysis, anything was possible. While waiting for the legal case to be set in motion, Madeleine suggested that she should find out how they went about things at the time. She suggested that she should call on the expertise of a funeral director, and that she would invite him to one of their next meetings.

In the following paragraph, the ambassador shamelessly writes that the Irish minister *knows nothing about* it, and even boasts of the favourable diplomatic benefits of the operation. He was thanked warmly by the Irish Minister of External Affairs. That takes the biscuit.

The Scattered listen to Madeleine, stifling their reactions in an offended silence, a silence that only the wind interrupts. The gruff southern wind growls in the old village cemetery and makes the dark branches of the umbrella pines dance. Madeleine distributes the investigative report quoted in the letter. It is signed by Paris's envoy. A certain 'Cailloux', meaning pebbles. You couldn't make it up.

William

Who is disturbing my bones, my dusty, badly buried poet's remains? Do they seek what I myself sought for a long time before finally obtaining it – a world stitched with dreams, the embroidered cloths of the heavens, reflecting the fate foretold in the cards?

Yes, for a long time I asked the tarot cards about the fate of my love, the rose that pricked my heart. I waited for the eternal voices to bring me news, to tell me if my beloved loved me in return. My feverish fingers spread the twenty-two cards upside down on the table, divinatory figures with their cheeks pressed against the mahogany where God's hand had become flesh in mine. I ceaselessly addressed my questions to the higher spheres and flung question marks into the deep blue sky.

Were my beloved to stop loving me, I preferred to imagine her dead, laid out, stone cold; then I could tell her everything,

I could kneel down and kiss her feet; I could finally die because of the death of my love. But my beloved was alive. My sweet Maud wrote to me, asking about my verses and Ireland. She spoke neither of love nor of roses; she allowed the thorn in my heart to dig its grave. She left me on the edge of the other world – dying, consumed by my own flame. I contemplated the divine will lying before me on my cards, on my cards arranged before me in the form of a cross.

I read the cards attentively, from left to right and from top to bottom. The first portrayed me as a juggler: I was the innocent, skilful juggler in a hilly landscape, he who, filled with the energy of desire, takes up his journey, in the place where another – perhaps himself, in a past life – could do nothing other than to lie down and wait. I thought this augured well, I was a young poet–suitor determined to conquer the queen and her kingdom, to take my share of the cake and eat it. I stood up to face the wind, determined to rise above my destiny through the force of my arms. Alas, my lanky limbs with their bulging veins would not take me far. I was inevitably slowed down by the next card, the one that examines the obstacles and warns of danger. Opposite the juggler was card number XV, 'The Devil' – inherited from the god Pan, son of Hermes and a nymph, with a hairy chest, goat's feet and horns and a curved nose and tail. He was so ugly that his mother abandoned him, so ugly that he was mocked by the gods of Olympus. Nevertheless, he was a seasoned seducer, a devourer of ephebes and goddesses, the slayer of ardour. It is said that one day the nymph Syrinx turned herself into a reed to escape his charms and cruel Pan turned the reed into a flute.

Centuries later, Christians called him the 'Devil', a creature with the appearance of a beast, with insatiable sensual instincts and irresistible magnetic power. This devil who sat on the table was my inner devil – he was in me like the genie is in the lamp; he was working on my innermost being, stirring up the bundles of misfortunes that were piling up on my chest, one by one, and turning them into impassable mounds. It is true that my weaknesses were mine alone; the devil only made use of them himself, made me his slave and pushed me to the bottom of the cauldron in which my unfulfilled passions soaked. My flesh harboured my worst enemy – an inner demon, an intimate demon – who nibbled at my heart and left the rest for my verses. For my poetry.

I resumed my reading and regained hope when I saw, above my head, 'The World' – the twenty-first blade – a huge crown of laurels in the centre of which a triumphant, naked woman was dancing on the back of a bull, celebrating a new beginning. The card was clear, I had the resources to fulfil my destiny – including love. Nothing less than a bull, a lion with a halo and a phoenix were at my service, all of which the tarot cards had foreseen would come to my aid and make me their laureate: a poet with ears full of whispers. But destiny, which always comes in fits and starts, floundered helplessly again with the next card – 'The Fool', a terrifying, simian character. The 'Fool', the 'Mate', was waiting for me on the other side of my torrent of glories, ambushing me on the invisible side of my pleasures, to make me pay. My happiness would go hand in hand with the insurmountable test of my unrequited love. It was a question of proportions, I suppose, of learned calculations on celestial ground. Alas, I was only a poet; I should have become a mathematician.

5

Madeleine is terribly out of breath; heaving but happy, she reaches the top of the hill in Saint-Pancrace cemetery, delighted in spite of everything to have reached the top so she can enjoy the spectacular panorama over the Riviera. The only flaw of this old seaside cemetery, this idyllic, high-perched place, is that there is no lift to bring people to the different levels. *It's a way to get rid of stout people like me,* she thought, *and old people, those who already have one foot in the grave here.* If they get fed up, they'll only have to go up and down the stairs. They'll already be on site, and will only have to lie down (if possible, in front of the right grave) to gaze at the most dazzling of landscapes one last time, before closing their eyes. However, this is not the object of today's visit. On the advice of the cobbler, she has come to see the caretaker, the man who has been coming and going among the graves for nearly twenty years and who knows the place like the pockets of his gabardine. From the very beginning of the affair Madeleine has been interested in cemeteries; she has learned about taphophilia – the study of tombs, funerary art and epitaphs – and about specialized tourism. She has read that enthusiasts visit famous graves, that there is a ranking of the 'best cemeteries', with the Parisian ones and the one in Lépanges-sur-Vologne, where poor little Gregory was buried, at the top of the list. Madeleine has stopped reading. No, the dead do not belong to everyone. To visit their graves you have to have known them, to be filled with their memory. Otherwise, what is it? Desecration. It has nothing to do with religion. For a long time Madeleine had flaunted her atheism to her grandmother, who always replied by saying: 'You'll come back to it, child, you may not be aware of it, but deep down you're on your way. You'll return to your faith, mark my words.' Although she is not heading in that direction (of this she is quite sure), Madeleine is nonetheless convinced that the bodies of the dead must be left whole, treated with the same dignity as those of the living. The story of the mass grave has aroused feelings of revolt in her. Nothing religious, though; on the contrary, *The less we believe in the soul, the more we believe in the body,* she says to herself – *It is the only tangible embodiment of the deceased and of their memory that we are duty-bound to honour.*

*

Carlo Veine, the caretaker

Hello, how are you today? Were you the one who wanted to see me, love? Nice to meet you. The registry office in

Roquebrune told me you were stopping by. What can I do for you? Watch out for the cat behind you, it has a way of getting tangled up in the visitors' legs. Do you like cats? You know, I ended up here because of a cat. The owner of a big villa was ill. She was in hospital and her son was looking for someone who would be willing to live there and look after the cat. It's weird, isn't it? But that's how I spent twelve years living in a beautiful villa. The owner had made her son promise to keep the estate open as long as the cat was alive. So I lived with him, so to speak, until he died. Cats are magical animals. As I love medicinal plants and gardens, I created a kitchen garden – I also have one at the back of the cemetery. The cat was called Mystic, he was a wonderful little ginger. When he died, I had to leave, of course, and the house was sold. A friend came to see me and said, 'I've been offered a job as a caretaker in a cemetery. I'm not interested in it at all. I don't want to be around death, but if you're interested, go for it, they're looking for someone.' I applied, and I took to it right away. And I still like it. You know, it's like a vocation. My mother was the only one who was unhappy – she used to say to me, 'Carlo, it's not good to work in a cemetery.' My mother was Sicilian. Her generation didn't talk about death. Even now, in France, we still don't talk about it. When I tell people that I'm a cemetery caretaker, they say, 'How horrible! So you see corpses?' Well yes, I see rotting corpses, when families are forced to move bodies around to make room inside a crypt, so what? People imagine absurd things, they ask me if the bodies have nails and hair that continue to grow, if they are full of maggots. Weird ideas. They've seen it on TV, I imagine. They don't understand my work. Sometimes I keep them guessing, I tell them that 'I look after the welfare of all those who have contributed to the town of Roquebrune-Cap-Martin', so people try to figure out what I do. And some of them do!

I'm interested in the dead and cemeteries. You know, I subscribe to a funerary magazine. It's fascinating to learn what happened in cemeteries in the Middle Ages, for example. They were convivial places, where the family could meet and talk about and remember the deceased. They were not places of mourning or grief at all. In the last issue of the magazine, there was a report on the first embalmers who came to France in the 1960s. They were American. They were the people who started to treat dead bodies so that they could be shown to their families in a presentable state. Did you know that? There are strict procedures to be followed in preparing a dead body for embalming. All the blood is removed and preservative fluid is injected into the body. In the old days, people used formalin, which was great but toxic; today its use is forbidden. Unfortunately, the new products are less effective and bodies have to be buried within six days. Otherwise, the level of decomposition is too great. Bodies start to rot very quickly, you know. After three hours, they already start to change. Unless they are kept in cold rooms. In people's homes, dry-ice packs are put under their backs. It's a relatively effective method. In the magazine, they explain all the different methods in detail, including the oldest ones. I find it fascinating. For example, did you know that the orifices of the dead used to be sewn shut to prevent the liquid from coming out?

Yes, everything was sewn shut – the anus, the vagina and the mouth. Later on, the orifices were plugged with cotton.

Today, everything is glued closed. Even the mouth and nostrils. Ah, yes, things have changed!

The worst thing about death, for me, is the nakedness of the body. And the fact that strangers are handling the body of your wife or your mother. Their privacy is no longer respected. There are no boundaries any longer. I find that completely unbearable. The rest – decomposition, all of that – doesn't bother me because in the end we are like plants. No more, no less.

I'm sorry, I'm getting distracted. To answer your question, I took up my post in the 2000s, and as you know the poet had already been exhumed long before then. The only information I can give you is the location of his grave. Would you like to see it?

Since his body was repatriated, all that is left is a stone in his memory, erected by one of his friends. The visitors, especially the tourists, are very happy to see it when they come to the cemetery – it's better than nothing. You know, people admire Yeats a lot. The other day a gentleman told me he was 'the greatest poet in the English language'. I'm often asked where he was buried. It's a good thing there are caretakers in the cemeteries. Otherwise, can you imagine what would happen? Over time, everything would be forgotten. I like the stone that commemorates Mr William Butler: it's rather flattering, the light-coloured marble with the unicorn, don't you think? I never understood why it had wings. A winged horse, I get, but a unicorn?

Why are you talking about a communal grave? Had he been buried before that? I didn't know. Why was that?

So just to be clear, when we talk about a communal grave, you need to know what the term means. Today, the term we employ is 'the plot for people without adequate resources'. Bodies end up there for one of two possible reasons – either they are buried there straightaway (most of the time for financial reasons) or they end up there later when the cemetery authorities take possession of neglected plots. Those are the two scenarios, love. Which one of them applies to Yeats? I can't tell you, I don't know.

You're right, in the ossuary, we don't keep the coffin, just the human remains – that is to say the head, the arms, everything that is 'solid', as we say in our jargon. Today, we separate each body so as not to mix them up, I can guarantee you that. What did they do at the time? I don't know. Because I have to tell you that in the 1940s the regulations on that question were still vague, to say the least – they certainly threw everyone in together. It is no longer the case, as the law governing local authorities came into force in 2005, obliging local authorities to 'arrange ossuaries in a suitable fashion'. We no longer put the bodies into the pit; we place them in reliquaries, little boxes with their names on them so that they can be found, you see?

What I don't understand about your Mr Yeats is why he ended up in the ossuary within a year when the law allocates a plot for at least ten years after burial. Something must have happened. So how were they able to identify his remains?

Ah, my pleasure, Madame, show me your document. I am interested in everything that has happened in my cemetery.

*

41

Madeleine gives the guard the report drawn up by Agent Cailloux in 1948, the result of the investigation carried out before Yeats's body was transferred. In deliciously bureaucratic language, Cailloux goes back over the circumstances of the death, which occurred on 28 January 1939, at the Ideal-Séjour hotel in Roquebrune-Cap-Martin. He admits that he cannot find any witnesses who were friendly with Yeats, only the owners of the hotel who had a vague memory of him, mentioning *his tall height, his large head and his paralysed legs*. The death certificate drawn up by the doctor only mentions the Bible that the poet was holding in his hands at the time of his death – not enough information to solve the mystery.

The agent had nevertheless managed to establish one certain fact: when Yeats's bones were transferred to the ossuary, they had been *mixed in with the remains of several people deposited in the same plot of the mass grave*. It was therefore impossible *to restore anything of absolute authenticity*, as Agent Cailloux himself agreed.

Cailloux wasn't prepared to give up. He got hold of the report from an investigation initiated by the family after they discovered that the body had ended up in the communal grave. He had learned that Yeats's remains were identifiable by an *iron corselet with retaining strips* and *an exceptionally large skull fitted with a dental prosthesis made from a modelling compound*. Cailloux concluded optimistically that partial identification was possible – a certain Rebouillat, a pathologist in Roquebrune, *would be able to put together a skeleton with all the characteristics of the deceased*. Delighted to have found a solution, Cailloux even gave a list of the addresses of recommended funeral parlours in Menton with *specialized personnel* who might carry out these searches. He had kept the Roquebrune *mairie* informed of the steps taken. Everything was in order.

'This is very serious stuff, Madame. Very serious indeed. It's not professional behaviour at all. Do you realize that?'

Madeleine does realize it. The caretaker's indignation reinforces her own. Strengthens it. She wonders how such goings-on could have happened. How the ancestors of the Scattered could have been used as coffin fodder without anyone taking offence.

William

I was the poet with the red rose and the golden cross. The follower of a secret society who drank the sacred rituals of the sun in a cup, caressed the soft moon and followed the paths that were bathed in its rays. The universe was in every drop of rain. I walked on unexpected and astoundingly divine peaks, from which I consumed a thousand lives parallel to my own. I followed the teachings of the masters until I became a cartomancer, a magician and an astrologer. I was religious in my own way: I trod the supernatural paths of Mathers, Westcott and the Celtic Movement. My mind became a cave filled with signs, sketches and poetry, with Eastern philosophy and ancient beliefs, with windows through which I could fly. I was part of all the journeys, of all those celestial or sunken worlds that opened my world, that gave me a view beyond my mere existence, that sent me to the moon or brought me back to Tír na nÓg, the land of Niamh, of Oisín and his wanderings.

Mathers called himself MacGregor. He taught magic and war. He taught me to make images grow like flowers, to let shapes and colours explode within me, to see as if in daylight when my eyes were closed. Mathers was the leader of our secrets, of our society of 'Hermetic Scholars', the inexperienced magicians that we were then, of whom dear Florence Farr, the dazzling actress and reader of poetry, was also a member. I devoured the manuals of the Theosophical Society and searched within myself for the Odic Force that Baron Reichenbach's treatises led me to believe in. The strength came not from my hands, but from my eyes. The images grew before my eyes as if blossoming from my eyelids. They crawled inside me, along unknown channels, and sprang up from behind the symbols Mathers gave me. I felt the splinters of the past, the ashes, the rags joining the silhouettes of the ancient dead, putting flesh on the backs of Titans again. Creatures came to me, straight out of paintings – horses crushing the fields of my consciousness with their hooves or living beasts let loose in the woods of my heart. I allowed what I was blind to in my soul come to me: the invisible forces that exist far beyond our bodies, beyond time, beyond our subconscious, and are at one with the universe – from the smallest grain of earth to the sap of the trees. Mathers lifted the veil. I felt the scent of incense completing the picture, drifting into visions more real than flesh, truer than I had ever thought possible.

6

Carlo Veine, the caretaker (continued)

On the subject of the records, I will tell you what I have been told, my dear lady. I warn you, I may disappoint you. In the beginning, the *mairie* was in the old village of Roquebrune. With the expansion that happened after the war, the *mairie* became too small and was moved to a new building. Unfortunately, the officials of the time threw away the old registers. More than a century of records, can you imagine that? They said, 'They're dead. They're dead, we don't need them anymore.' Can you imagine that? It's scandalous, but that's how it is.

Ah, I'm delighted that you found a record of Mr William Butler's death in the parish registers, Madame. I didn't know they were held in the library of Princess Grace of Monaco. Did you know that she was of Irish descent too?

Let me see … *Payment slip.* Yes, that's the fee you pay to the police when they seal the body before burial. It's normal procedure. But look, it says that he was buried on 28 January 1939 and exhumed on 7 February 1939 to be put in the depository. This is very strange, Madame. That means that he was transferred to the ossuary not after a year but a week after his death! That's incredible, because, you see, the depository is where you put the bodies awaiting burial. That means that they put him there while waiting to rebury him – but in the communal grave on that occasion. But why? I'm learning about this at the same time as you, love. What I'm going to tell you isn't nice, but at the time some people used to get preferential treatment when it came to getting a grave in the cemetery. Saint-Pancrace was full, and the new cemetery didn't exist. Yes, it's sad but true, Madame.

Show me the other forms. Yes, this is the one for the exhumation from the communal grave. It's dated 8 April 1948. As you can see, the fees were paid for the exhumation of several bodies. Not just the mortal remains of Mr William Butler. Look, they give four names. Why were those bodies exhumed from the ossuary? That is a good question.

And these are the measures taken for the transfer of the remains to Ireland. *24 November 1948* – that fits. *Assistance with the departure of the body of Mr Yeats William to be transported out of the locality, the transfer was unable to happen immediately after the burial.* To say the least!

You're welcome, my dear. Come back if you have any further questions, don't hesitate. You know where to find me.

*

Madeleine thanks the caretaker and promises to keep him informed of the progress of the investigation. She reaches the large staircase that leads to the cemetery exit and valiantly begins her ascent. Her knees are aching from standing for too long; her stiff legs look as if they are made from the same marble as the graves around them. There isn't one seat in the cemetery, not one bench to sit on. *Here it's either stand or lie down, no other choice,* she says to herself. Her courageous feet continue to climb the steps – those blocks of granite stuck together with concrete like Siamese twins. She takes a break every three or four minutes and breathes deeply. She walks slowly, but her heart beats fast, *the pressure will make it age quickly,* she thinks as she feels it throbbing inside her, knocking without her being able to do anything about it. Each level offers an unobstructed view. *You can see everything,* she says to herself – pretentious black tombs with shiny marble, some blazing red like torches, others adorned with a bust as if they were chapels, and also some raised graves, some covered in moss, others unreadable. Madeleine takes deep breaths as she gazes at them; she struggles up the steps – they are testing her, a contest between her willpower and the stones. She climbs slowly, repeating meditative phrases to herself over and over again that help her catch her breath. She is living in the moment, feeling gratitude for the cemetery, for her breath; she feels joy here and now, she is grateful for this moment she has been granted, she observes her emotions without being attached to them, she allows herself to dream and to be carried away. In her mind's eye, she creates effortlessly what

48

she desires. Now she is halfway there, she takes the time for contemplation, takes a break without thinking a single negative thought. *I am in harmony with the sounds and images around me.* Her gaze mechanically sweeps the surrounding graves, deciphers the plaques that lie upright or flat, the usual inscriptions: TO OUR DEAR UNCLE, FOREVER, MAY YOUR REST BE AS SWEET AS YOUR SMILE ... One of the larger, newer graves displays its golden letters like a mirror held up to the sun that looks down on it. She moves close to read. TO MY FATHER-IN-LAW, MY LIFELONG LOVER. The inscription seeps into her mind as if the author is whispering it in her ears. Madeleine turns this sentence over and over in her mind. Her train of thought comes to a screeching halt, unable to get over the striking confession, the revelation displayed on the tomb, making the visitor a witness to a hidden love. How many burning enigmas, unmentionable secrets, lurk in the shallows of the cemetery, hidden among the dead? 'To my father-in-law, my lifelong lover,' she repeats. This mantra is not for her. She already seen her share. She leaves it for someone else.

William

Through my telescope, I studied the stars up close. As an astrologer, I traced the squares, the trigones and the sextiles with a ruler. I discovered that I was the son of Mercury and Saturn; I saw terrifying Pluto tying up Venus, my loves, taking them off the beaten track; I could read my destiny in the stars like an open book.

I was born on 13 June 1865, at 10.40 pm, in Sandymount, Dublin. I was Willie the Gemini, with Capricorn rising, my poetry nestled in the third house of the zodiac, between Venus and Pluto, between the goddess of love and the god of the underworld. I was the one who had to write what he could not do, who had to build a kingdom of paper and erect an empire of verse. The affairs of the heart granted to me by Venus were held captive by the gaze of Mars, a warlike and brutal god. Without weapons or a helmet, I was thrown by invisible forces into frightening adventures, legends of love in the hills of the flat mountain, where the fog cries. I was an insatiable child of Sligo's landscapes, my sun, my refuge, from which Uranus, my rebellious and unpredictable planet, kept pulling me away. Yes, Uranus played tricks on me, often knocking me out of the nest, throwing me into an exile as futile as if I were spinning round on myself. Nonetheless, I came back to it every summer, as the animals come to the river every evening to quench their thirst. I sucked in its beauty, hugged its trees and ate its fruits, drank its rain and made it part of my physical makeup. Sligo was in all my thoughts, in all the loves I imagined dancing on the land at night in white dresses, women–druids who invoked the souls of the dead and lay on my heart to stop it beating.

The stars were very clear in their expectations – they wished me to fulfil my lyrical duty, my role as a poet. Jupiter was enthroned in my birth chart in the great eleventh house, the collective house – I had to obtain for others the freedom that I, fettered and enslaved to my talents, lacked; I was to draw a new Ireland on the sea, to float a liberated island on the page. As a child, forever clinging to the umbilical cord, feels very deeply the sufferings of its mother, so my woes melted into those of the island that had begotten me, sealing my fate to that of my land. Like Ireland's Robinson Crusoe, I brought to life under my pen the trampled stories of the heroes, of the riders Caoilte, Conan and Finn, of the slaughtered lying dead under the scavengers' paws on the plain of Gabhra. I sang of the loves of Oisín and Queen Maeve, I whistled up the hooves that carried her across the foam and I harvested the salt left on the earth. My mission was reduced to my page, I was the legendary poet of a nation whose language I did not know –

a tongue which had been excised from its ancestors, they had swallowed it and I spat it back in the face of the invader.

I had to fight against other planets, those concentrated in the north-east quadrant that favoured introspection. If I followed them, I would lock myself away in my tower, accumulating impressions to the detriment of adventure. As an armchair activist, I was armed with a pen of bright, wet ink that I fearlessly stuck into the abscesses of Ireland, to cure it.

Scorpio, Pisces, Cancer did not figure in my chart – I was a child of the air and the fire, reduced to a life without water, which had evaporated at my birth. I was chronically thirsty for love, and I jumped into an inferno of passions that I could not extinguish. I thought Maud, my dear Maud, was alone. She was not. Her lover was the horrible Lucien Millevoye, the anti-Dreyfusard, the old Boulangiste who inflamed the French parliament with his scapegoating violence, the man who wanted to reconquer Alsace and Lorraine. He converted Maud to his form of nationalism and his enemies, the English, became hers too. They stood up to them together – Maud and Millevoye united, hand in hand, like a shield against the crown, a two-headed hydra, with the French cockerel on the right and the Irish wolfhound on the left. Maud carried the cause of the Irish on her heroine's back; she made the names of the martyrs and the misfortunes of the oppressed people known beyond France. She brought the glorious past to the surface. Her tempestuous speeches crossed the sea, awakened the waves and currents and raised the bodies of the hanged men of the Kingdom. I reproduced Maud's speeches on the pages of *United Ireland*:

How can I make you see, how can I make you feel the wonderful past that lives forever in the hearts and memories of our race? Our dead illusions, our heroes, our martyrs, all that world of memories, of examples, of glories, of immortal deeds which England wants to bury in the grave, but which will one day rise up against her ...

The pages set my dry fingers ablaze, made me a raging torch whose conceited hope was to make Maud shine like a moonbeam on the vault of heaven, on the open roof of Ireland.

7

Jacques Diallo, undertaker

The episode always begins with an unusual death. Jacques
Diallo is anxious to know how it will happen. The two hands,
close-up on the screen, do not belong to the same person:
one is a man's, the other a woman's. They are both undeni-
ably wrinkled. They clasp together and then separate, very
slowly, which indicates that the thing is sad, no doubt about
it. The interlaced hands separate, gradually leave the field of
vision, one to the right, the other to the left, giving a glimpse
of a green, slightly hilly landscape, like you would find in
places as diverse as Corrèze, Provence (exclusively in spring)
or anywhere in Ireland (all year round).

Pay attention, there is a change of scene. This time the feet
are front and centre, so to speak. Although remarkably narrow,
their size leaves some doubt as to the sex of the individual to
whom they belong – belonged? The doubt as to the use of the

past tense is quickly dispelled: a label hangs from the (surprisingly graceful) big toe on the left foot. In the background, a threatening sky with clouds – perhaps the clouds are clearing (at least, that is one possible interpretation) – gradually giving the illusion of covering the feet, like a greyish shroud.

A small, shrill sound mingles with the music, indicating the movement of the trolley (its pivoting wheels tend to squeak). The same feet can be seen, still prominent, to the front of the trolley, as if pointing the way although there is only one possible way to go – down a long, narrow corridor to the exit, which is bathed in light. It's true that the shot could have been avoided; nonetheless, in this particular case it allows the viewer to move from the light at the end of the corridor to that reflected in the bottles of the embalmer at work. With very professional gestures, the embalmer applies a cotton pad to the face that is finally revealed and is, surprisingly … a dead woman. As her feet suggest, she is tall, delicately built and sublimely beautiful. The cotton wool caresses her brown eyebrows, revealing open eyelids and blue eyes of exceptional intensity that beautifully match her complexion, which is lighter than ever. The (immaculate) white of her shroud provides a subtle transition to the colour of the lily and lace curtain in the mortuary vehicle.

The film moves to the cemetery and cuts to the tombstones where – surely the height of sophistication – the names of the director and actors are superimposed to look engraved. In a rectangular frame, sunk six feet underground, beneath a tree, the name of the series appears. As the letters fade away, Jacques Diallo removes his lisle socks and stretches out his legs on the footstool. He has exactly enough time left to watch one episode before the first customer enters his shop.

William

I knew that Maud the rebel was free, free of all conventions, that she would have broken her ankles rather than allow any ball and chain to be attached to them. But I did not know that she loved Millevoye, that awful man who was married to someone else. She loved Millevoye, the former journalist and nationalist member of parliament; she loved him in spite of his embarrassing political positions, in spite of his musty smell and the fact that he was at the end of his political career. She saw him as an old king, with a bushy moustache; a Celtic chieftain from ancient Gaul, with an iron helmet, who was armed with a sling, an axe and a stone knife. She listened to him preach about the grandeur of France from atop his rock, declaiming his eternal refrain. At his side, Maud howled like a she-wolf. She howled for the story of exile and for her lost country, which had not yet been born.

In Ireland, Maud had fought for the poor. In County Donegal, she had untied tight purse strings; she had built roofs over the destitute, she had planted sharp stakes around their land. Maud had opened the cage with the sleeping birds of legend that were nesting the eggs of the world. She had pushed them out of the nest, she had ravished their sword-like feathers from which flowed the black ink of *L'Irlande libre* – her newspaper. Maud the Amazon, with her shamrock-covered bosom, had picked up the still-green leaves of independence. She had collected nationalist ballads and the Fenian poems of Ellen O'Leary. Ellen's verses told the story of tearful, proud lovers sitting on the graves of heroes buried with their weapons, who had died in prison for the Ireland of the future. Maud had made their names known; she had mixed sulphur and coal, spread the poetic black powder across the country-in-waiting and lit the fuse. As chief artificer, she had prepared for war. She had fought until the wind changed. She had waited for the steel of the bars to close in on her from all sides before fleeing. Maud had set sail, landed in France, taken refuge in the comforting arms of the City of Light and in those of Millevoye; she even bore him a child – Georges, the forbidden son.

I was unaware of the love affair of the beautiful woman and the old goat. Had I been aware of them my affection would have remained the same, for Maud was not human. She was my Maud, above all else, the fairy queen sitting on top of Ben Bulben, the mountain of my childhood; she was wrapped in the fabric of my dreams and could not be removed. She was in an unattainable position, a place where no one could reach her. I had created the place where my love was lying, with my closed eyes – a flat mountain covered with green that offered her masterly silhouette the comfort of moss, the warmth and light of a sky within reach. Not a branch, not a leaf obstructed the divine rays that the sun, which was also dazzled by her, traced in straight lines towards the fairy queen, recharging her powers forever. Maud was nourished by this sun that I imagined for her. She would be intoxicated when it was at its zenith, would capture the light, would shine it from her chest until it overflowed into a sacred ring set in gold that radiated out of her. The aura which then burst forth from Maud had the vigour of the fire of Moses' bush; like it, she was not consumed by the fire. She was calling me, imploring me to remove my sandals, to kneel on the now-holy ground beneath her feet and lay my rhymes down before her. Then my vision would blur, Maud would strip herself of her shell; she would evaporate, melt into the mountain wind and scatter into ashes. I was ready to fall, to jump from the heights of the flat mountain, to feel Maud's hands in the winds that caressed me as I fell. Words came at the fatal moment as I held my breath, as I drowned in my tears, as I bent my knees for the final leap, making a sacrifice to love. I always seemed to hear an oracle between my temples at the last minute, announcing the return of my love, a voice that shattered my reason, seeped into the broth of my blood and flesh and despised the obstacles I faced. Sometimes the oracle came from Maud herself. She wrote to me: 'I shall certainly be in Ireland on the 31st of July,' her tone was sad and tender; she would reveal a dream – perhaps a past life, in which we were brother and sister, both slaves sold in Arabia. I knew nothing of her ordeals in France, I asked for her hand without reading her palm; I followed the oracle of my thoughts blindly, the thread of my destiny as a cursed lover. Maud did not give me her hand, she closed it over her secrets. My love was left in my rhymes; it swirled indefinitely around her, tied the perpetual escapee to the page. I abandoned the idea of jumping; I sat over the chasm, on the sacrificial tripod, let the oracle descend into me and run across the page. I did not understand the prophetic breath of my inner Pythia, which spoke of Maud, roses, white birds and the Ireland to come. I knew nothing except that she was taking me back to my beloved to save me from dying.

8

The beanpole is in his car, driving along the road between Roquebrune and Menton, going to the pharmacy where he works every day from 9 am to 7 pm. He calmly negotiates the bends while glancing at the dating app on his phone where toned bodies and protruding torsos appear in close-up. On his profile, the beanpole has his back to the camera and his smooth skin is highlighted by sepia tones. In the accompanying text, he has posted his situation: *single, looking for an open relationship or a throuple*. At each traffic light, a mosaic of profiles appears before his eyes – *bears*, well-built, hairy bears; *the discreet*, whose homosexuality remains hidden; *sportsmen*; the *well-groomed*; *twinks* like him etc. He clicks on a bust acting as a support for a huge bird, a grey-green mocking crow whose wings spread out over swollen pecs. The beanpole himself is tattooed from head to toe with tiny Chinese characters – from a distance they look like spots, giving him the allure of a panther. The fresco keeps growing over time; whenever he can, he goes back to lie down in the gloomy salon, lets the needle cover his sadness. They call back to himself, to his flesh that seems so often foreign to him. Tattooing always heals him, brings him back to life in spurts, gives him a chance to redefine his contours once again. Alas, it is too early, the mockingbird is not yet online; the beanpole continues on his way. He parks in front of the funeral parlour, which he has not visited since the death of Louise, his maternal grandmother. Whereas the other deceased family members died at home, wisely staying in their rooms until their funerals, Louise ended her days in hospital. She was taken to a funeral parlour, to the special room provided for families so as to spare them the presence of the dead and the exhausting visits. The beanpole remembers the sickening smell of lacquer and perfume from this last tête-à-tête, the image of a thick, plum-coloured carpet on which his Italian shoes left long, pointy prints. He didn't recognize Louise herself on that day – she had been prepared by the staff, her hair was done up strangely, her curls had disappeared and her hair was a uniform, puffy, silvery ball. The overly bright red lipstick gave her a look she would have been furious about if she could have made her voice heard from inside her coffin. Poor Louise. Her dead body was nothing like her. The features of her gaunt face were disappearing at a rate of knots. *The older people are, the faster the body decays*, the embalmer had explained. There was not much left of her, his eccentric grandmother disguised as a member of the bourgeoisie. Only her hands, perhaps, scratched with cemetery flowers. And the silk scarf knotted over her gold chain. The beanpole was sorry that he had given into the temptation of the final visit, sorry he had gone to see her up close, sorry he had felt the human husk with his hand. It now seemed to him that granny's substitute, lying in her luxury coffin, was waiting for him to leave the room so she could call him a miserable vulture. His cousin Gilles had encouraged him to go to see her, to say a final goodbye. 'You'll see how peaceful she looks,' he said. Thanks a bunch, Gilles.

At least she had had a nice funeral, with a high mass and eulogies given by her grandchildren, all decked out in their finery. The pallbearers had slowly dropped her coffin down alongside the other horizontal tenants of the crypt; below her lay the whole family. Only Louise's father was absent, missing since 1916. He and his fellow soldiers had been killed by shrapnel. Nothing remained of the trenches, the bodies, even their names. In the summer of 1922, when the war itself had been buried for years, the bodies of shattered soldiers were repatriated to Roquebrune. No identification of the individual bodies had been possible; they had been buried together, thrown anonymously into a common grave. What do we know today about those sacrificed youngsters, the soldiers who died in oblivion? Who were exiled to another front? Mobilized in their sleep for a diplomatic war? Thank God, Louise will never know.

The beanpole pushes open the door of the Divinatorium a few minutes after it opens. The place is flowery, furnished with a grandiose, plumped-up sofa on which he sits, waiting for the owner to finish his phone call, to free himself from the customer bellowing through the receiver: *One hundred euros a letter? You don't give a damn. It's discrimination! Is it my fault that my father was called Randrianampoinimeria?*

The beanpole picks up a leaflet from the dove-grey lacquered table itemizing the professions of those who deal in death – pallbearers, stone-carvers, masters of ceremonies and funeral advisers. He lingers on the specificity of each task, one article is devoted to the laying of crypts. He contemplates the photos of the construction site and the digger small enough to squeeze through the alleys of the cemetery, the workers with their bulging muscles. One of them holds on to the hook of the crane, guiding a concrete block down to the bottom of a tomb. The colossal operation has something anachronistic about it – the man hanging from the rope binds his fate to the stone, and buries himself with it six feet under. Do the privileges and the calling of the profession involve being buried and then rising again? Do they experience, multiple times, the turmoil of an individual's journey to their final resting place, an experience that is usually unique? No doubt about it, you need to be tough.

The funeral director comes in and distracts the beanpole from his inner preoccupations. He is dressed in a fashionable, slim-fitting black suit, a closely cut white shirt that suits his streamlined body, steel cufflinks with two black teardrops in the centre and suede boots – his elegance befits the occasion, and the beanpole is not insensitive to his charms. He agrees to answer the questions of the Scattered – 'it's not often that people are interested in our work' – and sits down next to him. On the left-hand side of the sofa.

9

Jacques Diallo, undertaker (continued)

To answer your question, in a crypt, the dead are in their coffins and there are tiers where the coffins are arranged in tight, circular rows. In contrast to what used to be called a mass grave, where the bodies were thrown unceremoniously into a single hole, and sand was put on top of them, and that was it.

Oh no, I won't deny that when a body had to be exhumed from those places, it was really very complicated to determine whether we had the right remains. Sometimes we found an item of clothing or a piece of jewellery that gave us information about the dead person, but that was entirely accidental. Otherwise, after a while, all dead people look the same.

Yes, of course, we had registers with the list of bodies and so on. But you have to bear in mind that, apart from its absolutely unquestionable economic advantage, a mass grave was designed to keep secrets. Those of the dead as much as those of the living. It concealed the failures and shameful deaths. All of those things were thrown into quicklime and then into the grave. Not to mention the crimes of all kinds. It doesn't bear thinking about, all of the things that can be found in there. It's like a mineshaft, a pit of stories, a mystery box, I tell you. Scores settled and concealed as suicides? Thrown in the pit. Infanticides disguised as accidents? Thrown in the pit. Shotgun blasts, which killed people accidentally during a hunt? Thrown in the pit. Everything was stuffed in a big hole and closed up. The bowels of the earth are very generous – they swallow everything up. It's like a natural regulation of sorts at the end of the food chain. It goes without saying, the pit is remarkably useful. And then, in the pit, we also put the paupers and the unidentified people; what else is to be done with them? Then we plant a tree or a flower next to it, symbolizing the dead. It's better than nothing.

Yes, when there are groupings of bodies, these are supposed to be noted in the registers by the cemetery caretakers. This has always been done in France. [*Sound of mobile phone ringing*] Sorry. Yes, hello, Prince? [*Pause*] Yes, I've been away because Marcel died. [*Pause*] Ah, right. What time do you finish? [*Pause*] Let's meet tonight, shall we? [*Pause*] See you later. Sorry, what we were saying?

Can a body be reconstructed from a skull? What method would you use, and how long after death would it be done? That's the main question. If you ask me, it's tinkering. Maybe our ancestors had their own methods of identifying bones, but they certainly weren't able to reconstruct a complete skeleton, especially once it had been mixed up with others in a grave. It's impossible, especially after nine years. Only the bones remain. Not to mention the fact that in the pit the bones are scattered. So how do you know what belongs to so-and-so? Can you imagine how many bones there are? All sizes of them! A phalanx, for example, find out who owns a phalanx. Of course, for some years now, we have been able to use DNA analysis, provided that there are still usable cells. But we can never reconstitute a whole skeleton; that, sir, I can guarantee. At best, we gather a few large bones – a skull, a femur – and return them to the family to bury. That's about it. It's more symbolic than anything else.

But I will tell you all about it in detail when we meet your friends. May I make a note in my diary? When is your meeting scheduled?

William

When I saw Maud again it was in the shadow of Parnell's coffin, at the funeral of the uncrowned king. Nationalist Ireland was in mourning, so was Maud. Her child, her secret French son still in his swaddling clothes, was gone. *Gone.* Maud couldn't get over it. Furiously she breathed in the chloroform from her handkerchief to chase away the darkness, to find the face with its round features and full cheeks, to sleep. She begged for magic to revive the tiny body, before the thin earth swallowed it up and kept it trapped in its womb. She believed herself to be Isis collecting the fragments of Osiris, scattered all over Egypt, so as to entrust them to the sacred rituals of Nephthys, Thoth and Horus, who would bring him back to life. Maud was an Egyptian; she had the body embalmed and a chapel built to the glory of the son. Her soul was seized with visions in which a grey woman had the blood of a child on her hands. Her grief as a mother was endless, like a desert in which she wandered barefoot, sinking deeper into the sand with every step until a sandstorm came and buried her alive. Maud saw her past lives in which she had sinned, in which she had stood beside an Egyptian priest, her lover, who, in order to enrich himself, had uttered false oracles. He had brought the curse of God upon her and her son. She had paid the highest price with her own flesh. Her child had been sacrificed like the ram on the mountain and was not saved in extremis. God had not granted him, as he did Abraham, the grace of the angel. God had taken the knife himself, had slit the child's throat and, even worse, had inflicted a pain on her that tormented her skull so much that it quenched her spirit. My comrade Russell, the poet, would join us for long séances, asking the spirits if George could breathe again. Russell thought he might be reincarnated as a new child of the family. Two years later, Maud asked her former lover Millevoye to join her in the chapel at Samois built for their dead son. There they conceived another child.

I performed rites to the glory of the moon, which was my star. I called upon it when my mind's eye was empty. I united the moon with the earth and saw a curtain of light arise from this union, with flaming draped feet caressing the pastures and a flock of heads two hundred and twenty thousand miles above this world. The curtain was overhung by the archangel Gabriel, the angel of the moon and the divine messenger. I had heard of a ritual to be performed between the new moon and the following one, to invoke the protection of the arch-angels, to cover oneself with their wings, for the duration of the phase of the moon. They were each master in their own domain – Gabriel was the great guardian of love, clairvoyance and speech. I admired the medals that bore his seal; I saw them around the necks of my companions. They showed two moons surrounding a strange candlestick and four crosses – a talisman for the artists to protect their message. To summon the archangel, one had to set up the candles after the full moon and turn to him with a cup of water from which he could draw strength. The wish was to be transmitted to him in the form of a word drawn with a feather, which he would then use as an ambassador to the higher authorities. I kept tracing the four letters of my beloved's name to cure her of her suffering. I wrote verses in which a *holy future* called to her. George did not return, but she had a new angel: Iseult. Her name contained all the promises of the dawn, since her name meant that God was protecting the house.

10

Sitting in front of his awl, a brown boot in his hands, the cobbler takes the heel off and scrapes the damaged sole. What he likes most is filling in the hollow material, sticking on the custom-cut sole and hammering in the nails with a bang. 'It's really enjoyable,' he says, 'the rest is sewing.' No sooner has he said this than the needle begins to bite into the new sole, making beautiful, regular stitches. A few more hammer blows and he's there. He adds some final flourishes, starts polishing the boots and other pairs needing attention, listening to the voice that filters from the radio and fills the workshop. It tells of a twenty-year-old case that has remained unsolved.

A girl, after her mother's death, discovered a secret gallery under the well in the garden leading to a cabin. A shed buried seven metres underground, connected to the electricity supply, was furnished like a maid's room. A corpse lay under a pile of books on a mattress on the floor, a skeleton in garter belts and women's underwear. The voice on the radio says that the identity of the deceased is not known, but everything suggests that the body is that of the son of the family, who disappeared in 1991 without a trace. The pathologist takes the microphone and reports on the protocols in place to *make the skeleton talk*, to determine the circumstances of the death. The X-rays provided information, indicating that he was a man of average build, aged about thirty. The expert looked for any clues or signs that could identify the deceased – anomalies, old fractures, dental implants. He also examined the insects in the room, and their cycle of development, to establish the day and time of death. He used all scientific means available to him and carried out DNA analysis on the bones.

While awaiting the results, the police delved into the lives of the owner of the house, the mother and her son, gradually filling in the gaps in the story, trying to solve the suffocating mystery of the ghost, done up as a woman, hovering over the local inhabitants. The mother was a much-loved teacher, a model schoolmistress with one blot on her record – during her first year at the village school, aged twenty, she had given birth, although no one had known she was pregnant. No one had dared to question her, and no one learned anything more about the story. The son had gone to school with the other pupils and had lived with her until he disappeared.

The Ministry of the Interior had issued a search notice, but to no avail. The case remained unsolved for fifteen years, until the day the well was opened to reveal its macabre secret. Rumours still circulate, and everyone has their own theory – they all suspect the mother and accuse her of the crime. Did she know about the existence of the underground dwelling?

Did she leave her son to die there? How could it be other-wise, some say? Others say worse things, say that the woman was stout and could never have reached the underground dwelling. While the programme has not yet revealed the results of the tests (no spoilers), everyone is convinced that it must be the son's corpse. Who else could it be at the bottom of a well in her garden? The cobbler imagines the woman, the mother hen nesting on her child's grave, looking after him. Did she believe he had disappeared? Or, without daring to say it, without daring to believe it, had she noticed her son moving in the entrails of the earth, as she had when she was pregnant with him without anyone knowing? And what had happened to the dead man? Was it an accident? Did he electrocute himself while indulging in shameless sexual plea-sures involving electricity and garter belts in his boudoir? Had he buried himself with the intention of ending it all, and staying under his mother forever? A psychoanalyst has taken over from the expert and interprets the shrunken room as a giant womb in which the unwanted son, who might have been conceived after a rape, withdrew from the world for eternity. Music is playing, it gets faster and then comes the big reveal. The DNA results have spoken, and after a twen-ty-year wait they have proved that the corpse is indeed that of the son, who died in the grave he had built for himself. The oldest mysteries are safe no more, and one day they will all be solved.

The cobbler knows what he has to do, what he has to say. He hopes that the bones in Yeats's coffin are not too old, that the cells are still usable and that they too will speak. Is it madness to believe that Ireland would allow the exhumation of its greatest poet? Is it madness to imagine that France would move heaven and earth for a handful of dust? Certainly, it was to be expected that new obstacles would be erected for them over which they would have to jump. The battle would not take place on equal terms, it would be a David-and-Goliath encounter. Yet he knows he will not back down. Until the dead are returned to their loved ones, until men make amends for their errors, until the ghosts return to the land they had chosen as their final resting place, the living will wander with their hands covered in their remains. A new meeting had to be called. As soon as possible.

William

In Celtic legend, two men, Mark and Tristan, are madly in love with Iseult. To reconcile them, King Arthur decides that one man will have her as his lover when the trees are covered with leaves, and the other when they are without leaves. Mark chooses to be the winter husband, to enjoy the longer nights. Iseult, daughter of my beloved, was predestined – she too would be a coveted queen.

Maud joined the hermetic society. Between herself and myself, a secret alliance was sealed; my eyes gazed into the deep shadows that clothed her mourning face. I kissed her red, sad lips, I devoured her grief; I sucked in the death that flooded the goddess's heart before it took her over. I felt her come back to life. First, there was a feverish, drowning breath, then a sound, an unforgettable whisper, an incredible 'yes'. Maud said Yes. Yes to my love wandering in the stars, sitting on Sirius, legs dangling, trying to pull her towards a cloudless pink sky. I thought she was available, on offer. Alas, Maud's flame passed through me like the hand of a ghost. It passed through me to touch the forces of the afterlife and the stars. I was the lover of the occult to whom marriage is refused, the poet whose magic unites him with his beloved. I played with the spirits that played with me, I became both Hamlet and the spectre that beckoned to him, King of Death, as it were.

With my comrades – O'Donoghue the editor, the writer Rolleston and the poet Todhunter – we formed a literary society to write the library of *Young Ireland*. Maud was on board, lending her sweet eternal reading voice to the cause, and she toured France for it. The siren's song echoed like nothing else on earth. It was a high, lonely melody that lifted the sand from the depths of the sea, seeped into the souls of sleeping travellers and stirred their old hearts.

Like Maud and magic, poetry and Ireland were one. They existed in me like juice in the fruit and I pursued them as my deepest quests. I was the mystical poet with a dark face, often alone among my fellows, considered too Fenian to be honest. My words were carried by winds from Europe, variable winds, they were not heard – I was Willie the ghost before ever I died. The alchemy was in my verses. I resurrected Celtic voices and trod the paths of the peaceful druids where my dreams of gold melted into those of King Fergus. Fergus, King of Ulster, who loved Princess Ness, who did not love him back. As she had a son, Conchobar, whom she wished to raise to the snowy heights of power, she agreed to the marriage. Her condition was that Fergus should make him his worthy successor. He was to pledge his throne to her for one year. He would then ascend to it with the same ease. Mad Fergus entrusted his crown to her out of love. It never returned to his noble head.

II

Business never stops for Jacques Diallo, for one obvious reason – people die all day every day, including weekends. So he has to respond to requests from families, greet them, organize the funeral and help them choose funeral products, all of which often takes a considerable amount of time: 'Most mourners know nothing about the wishes of the dead.' His day is punctuated by constant trips to collect the bodies from retirement homes, hospitals or private houses. He then entrusts them to the embalmer for conservation care – at least there he can rest easy, his associate is an outstanding professional. There is also the administrative hassle, death notices and paperwork to be sorted out before the services can be delivered. He runs around non-stop until his mission is accomplished, until the coffin or urn is placed in the grave or the ashes are scattered in a suitable place. On this point, the law reinforcing the conditions for the exercise of the profession of a funeral operator has made his task much more difficult. Ashes, which have obtained the same legal protection as bodies, can no longer be kept: they must be buried or scattered. Relatives have to be reasoned with and reminded to obtain permission from the local authorities so that, while they cannot keep the urn, they can at least bury it in their garden, under a tree or in a flower bed. It's such heartbreak for them not be allowed to keep them close to hand, in a box, as part of the furniture. They get into dreadful states.

Some people make requests that still surprise him. Just last week, a client insisted that his wife's ashes be scattered, by drone, over the forest. Then, there were the wealthy American clients who came to enjoy a peaceful retirement on the coast. Jacques Diallo could not believe his ears when they asked for a space funeral.

Nothing of the sort happens at the Divinatorium, which does not go in for gimmicks. However, Jacques Diallo has taken advantage of the geographical situation by making the scattering of ashes at sea one of his specialities. In general, he advocates for what he calls 'funeral planning', a tailor-made funeral that reflects the life of the deceased. He has seen so many failures in his early career, so many one-size-fits-all funerals. At least the sea ceremonies he offers are meaningful to the locals. They connect them to the natural environment. Jacques Diallo offers two types of service – a traditional scattering three hundred metres from the Mediterranean coast or a complete immersion of the ashes in water, using a biodegradable urn made of clay or salt. To carry out the operation, he calls on the services of professional skippers. Sitting at the back seat of the boat, the families are quietly led to the authorized maritime zone where they can pay their respects and throw a wreath or a spray of flowers into the sea. For his part, Jacques Diallo acts as Master of Ceremonies and reads the appropriate verses. 'Soirée en mer' is the perfect poem, in which Victor Hugo tells of the two attitudes displayed by man when facing his inescapable destiny: bending his 'head to the worried wave' or raising a calm gaze 'to the starry hope'. He also sometimes recites Verlaine's 'Marine', with its sonorous ocean and 'mourning moon'. There is no shortage of quality writing about the sea, which is, given the circumstances, the best memorial there can be, one final blast of poetry before reaching the other side. Jacques Diallo often thinks of those ashes whose final resting place is the sea and which, united by tidal pull, experience a second life with the rocking of the waves, until gravity catches up with them and drags them down, drowning them after their death.

This morning he arrived at the Divinatorium at 7.30 am, time to prepare the display cases, rearrange the plaques and interments by colour, as he has decided to do, and place the personalized medallions he has just received on small velvet pillows. The clock is ticking, the employees will arrive soon. As usual, he is checking the cleanliness of the cups and the tea and coffee supply in the rest and meditation room. The text message that makes his phone vibrate stops him in his tracks.

Reminder: Scattered meeting
Time: 9 am
Location: Saint-Pancrace Cemetery
Travel time: 22 minutes

He pushes the armchairs and the sofa a couple of centimetres closer to the dark wooden floorboards and rushes away with a pile of brochures from his business in his hand. *You never know.*

*

Twenty-two minutes later, to be exact, Jacques Diallo greets the Scattered, all of whom he is meeting for the first time, with the exception of the beanpole, of course, who briefly introduces Diallo. At a glance he assesses the group, as he usually does with his clients – men and women belonging to the three categories outlined by the Institut National d'Études Démographiques: 20–59 years old, 60–64 years old and over 65 years old, most of them from Roquebrune's middle classes and from the surrounding area. He greets them courteously, shows his support for their approach and, before turning his attention to the communal grave, launches into a general presentation of his profession.

'Our working conditions are extremely difficult – as we deal with sadness and mourning and we take the psychological shocks of the families head on. And of course, there is physical hardship as people are getting heavier and heavier, and, in our region, the cemeteries are located on slopes and are accessed via stairs. We have no choice but to carry the coffins. I can assure you that our backs take a beating. I must also tell you that we work a lot. We deal with the transfer of the dead to the funeral home all the time, day and night, on weekends and public holidays. Between road accidents and homicides, there are always emergencies. It's a much more difficult job than it seems, I can assure you.'

Sensing that the audience is impatient to get to the subject that affects them directly, Jacques Diallo decides to address the issue of body conservation. The fate of a corpse in its natural state is to deteriorate rapidly, he explains, so professionals are in a race against time right up to the funeral. The tricky nature of pre-burial operations puts the staff at risk of contamination of various types, from microbes to viruses (hepatitis A, rota virus) or bacteria. 'You may be familiar with the words of the philosopher Paracelsus, who said that everything is toxic and nothing exists without toxicity ... Preservation also requires that the cold chain should not be broken.' Jacques Diallo then goes on to describe the daily difficulties faced by funeral specialists, 'with a concern for respecting human dignity, because the corporeal form of the deceased is their last shelter, the last thing we can take care of before letting them go'. He is now hot. He pauses slightly, takes off his jacket, folds it carefully in half, shoulder pad to shoulder pad, and lays it flat on the bench behind him, before going on: 'I don't know if you've heard about what happens in some medical institutions for example? A disgrace!' He angrily recalls a scandal reported in the newspapers a few weeks earlier. Bodies generously donated to science are sometimes left to rot – 'There's no other word for it' – in the basements of medical schools, the remains abandoned in rooms that are no longer cold, until rats nibble the blackened limbs. He describes the garbage bins overflowing with organs and chiselled flesh, where the dead are treated like rubbish – waste placed in the waste disposal with the grey plastic of the garbage bag as a coffin and the red string added as a final flourish. The corpses are cut up for experiments and then left lying on the floor in an unbearable scattering of head-less bodies, heads without trunks, staring up at the blinding neon lights of the dilapidated laboratory ceiling. Bodies are jumbled together, an arm placed on a neighbouring torso, a hand lying on a stranger's stomach. Sometimes the corpses are piled up, side by side, placed head to toe like bald mannequins stored in the lock-up of the showroom once the collection is sold. Sometimes their anatomical parts may themselves become subject to illicit trade. He knows that whole bodies are occasionally rented out for car-crash tests and crushed post-mortem. There are scientific profanations of all kinds, in return for payment, which take no account of the laws or the sacred dimension of the human body. 'This has been seen even in the biggest donation centres in Europe,' he adds. 'Medical students also play games of jacks with the bodies and that's not the worst. I've heard of hazing that consists of cutting off a dead man's penis and encouraging students to slip it under their scrubs. These people simply forget that the deceased was once a living person like them.' No, the dead don't always get the respect they deserve, and in this divide his struggle lies, as a professional, 'as a citizen and as a man', he insists.

The cobbler catches every crumb of Diallo's speech, Madeleine, who is hidden behind him, grabs her headphones and slips them discreetly over her ears. 'Romeo and Juliet' rings out, each of its notes essential to chase away the images that Diallo's words summon. His words make her sick. It must be even worse in the pit, in the hole, where the bruised bodies are piled up, contaminating each other, decomposing on top of each other. She looks at the cemetery and gazes at the stones buried up to their bellies. The dead are there underneath; it seems to her that they are gathering their scattered bones in one last effort to get out, to rise to the surface. There are so many of them trying to get out, allowing Madeleine to imagine their appearance and their past – the anonymous, the excommunicated, the destitute. There is also the youngest child in the mass grave, her grandmother Jeanne's baby, forever tiny – an eternal infant – who would have been her aunt, had she lived. Her grandmother never said anything about the dead baby, even though she had raised Madeleine as if she were her own; Madeleine's mother had died so young that her voice was lost in her memory, just like her face, blurred by time. No, Jeanne had never been able to say anything about it, not even to Madeleine. Her lips had remained closed, sealed by the knot that still gripped her heart, shut even tighter by the fear of remembering. Yes, the hiding place was sealed, and nothing would have made Madeleine aware of the loss except, perhaps, her grandmother's habit of always saying 'she' when referring to a baby. Madeleine had noticed that without giving it any further thought. Were there no other clues? Yes, Jeanne had loved Madeleine as if she were her daughter – as if she were the daughter she never had. Not living.

Baby Madeleine's tacit adoption had happened in silence. Her grandmother had taken on the role left vacant by a sick mother who had laid dying on the bed after the baby was born. Her grandmother had taken the neglected child in her arms, carried her for hours and rocked her to sleep in her arms. Her mother – her real one – had looked at them with gratitude. She had closed her eyes in peace. Her child was in the best of hands. Her grandmother's love had not been long coming; it had sprung from her old heart, warming the almost orphaned child whose mother would soon be gone. A generation later, death had reversed the roles; the mother died, leaving the child and offering Jeanne the opportunity of motherhood in old age, of an unhoped-for redemption. Admittedly, a few years after the death of her stillborn daughter, Jeanne had a son, but it was not the same. When Madeleine was born it was as if the child had been resurrected and she finally had a daughter. Although no one dared to say it. Just as no one dared to admit that the sick woman in the bed had given up on being a mother. This secret was kept as well as that of their aunt who was hidden in limbo and died in secret. All the strings had remained tightly tied, lacing together the generations. After Madeleine was born, her grandmother stayed silent and said nothing to free the memory of the dead baby in the communal grave. Nor had she told anyone about the pain that had preceded it: the feeling of collapse in her womb, the loss that had taken hold in a confused way while the weight was still there, inside. The dead weight. Jeanne had immediately guessed that the baby was dead, she understood it long before it was explained to her; everything had come to a standstill. She had felt the absence weighing on her and growing ever more important, she knew that death had wreaked havoc on her womb. There was no more underwater swaying on either side, no more raised fists under her belly, there was nothing at all; her once-full body had suddenly been abandoned. She was pregnant with a form of emptiness, and so she had killed the story forever. She felt silently guilty for having carried death, for having been jinxed. One day Madeleine came across the birth certificate, handwritten with a civil servant's pen. And the secret was revealed to her, and she was finally able to pierce her grandmother's thick layer of grief and solitude and learn the story. Madeleine had also kept silent, she had gently closed the door behind her, on Jeanne's child, forever asleep.

Who dared to stir up the ashes of the innocents? Who dared to open the earth and its entrails? And all this for what? To fill an empty coffin? To please a minister? This plundering of the grave was not to go unpunished under any circumstances, this baby had only had a body – not even a name on the register – no one had the right to take it away. According to the testimonies gathered by Madeleine from family and friends, the child had died in the seventh month. Jeanne had given birth to death the next day, in her own bed, her tears joining the blood that soaked the rough linen sheets. This was not the pretty sickness that midwives talk about, the sickness that gives way to happiness when the child appears. Once the inert infant had been delivered, instead of disappearing the pain had become immeasurable. The pain had increased, had shaken her loins forever, had consumed her to the end. The pain that had started inside her was unquenchable, a life sentence. Jeanne had screamed so much – in grief, in pain – that the doctor had insisted she stay in bed and not attend the funeral. Deprived of the last sight of her daughter-dust, Jeanne had remained frozen in absence, at the gates of death that she had not seen close. The stone had fallen like a lid on the grave – without her. When she heard the news, Madeleine thought of St Luke, of his gospel she had heard read so many times during the endless masses of her childhood: *when the women from Galilee came to the tomb, the stone had been rolled away. They did not find the body of Jesus.* The body of the child had also disappeared. No resurrection awaited her, no miracle, only a plundering. Of unparalleled violence.

The cry of a bird of prey snaps Madeleine out of her thoughts. Jacques Diallo is still standing in front of them, continuing his speech; he has visibly branched off into ecological issues, the ins and outs of which Madeleine is not sure she understands: 'As you may know, we still have a lot of trouble substituting formaldehyde with organic products that are suitable for the proper preservation of bodies ...' She turns up the volume, no more words. Music is at this very moment the only language she can hear. That her body can bear.

William

Our country was not yet itself, it was a dough to be kneaded, a green fruit that we, members of the Young Ireland revolutionary movement, hoped to ripen and taste. With *The Nation* was born the struggle's journal of Gaelic literature; we put Young Ireland above all else, above God and the dogmas that had split our island, that had cut off its arms and bent its knees. Maud became a Catholic and was baptized in France like a queen. I was a Protestant like Synge, and like him I found myself among the Catholics of Ireland, those who knew the secrets of the earth, the living, hard roots of the birch, hazel and yew trees; those for whom the trees made up the ogham alphabet, from which the druids of Sligo once extracted divinatory sticks. They threw them on the ground, and as they fell the sticks performed a premonitory dance; it was said that through them the wise men knew what wood the future would be made of. Destiny was also read in their fruit; the hazelnuts fell into the waterways and formed mystically inspired bubbles on the surface. In Ireland, the land is covered with sacred woods that belong to all; their pagan spirits hover indiscriminately over our heads, above warring religions.

I was bewitched by Maud, my woodland goddess, surrounded by wild animals. No matter how much she rebuked me, no matter how much she pushed away the hand ready to take hers, she was always there. She haunted my thoughts like a woman from the other world, a transparent, supernatural creature who passed through me. Her voice kept the whisper of her insolent beauty in my ear. I heard her utter the eternal magic words, 'my dear Willie', 'always your friend'. Maud's friendship came to my soul like the eagle to the crow and laid its stupendous power upon me, a poor, black creature; it broke my spine with a great flapping of its wings. I was overwhelmed and used the last of my strength to raise my beak and flee with my feathers streaming. I flew with my wings half-broken and allowed myself to be carried by the gentle winds. I landed in other arms, which had the rounded strength of first love. A physical love.

Olivia was English, and her name was Shakespear. Her marriage was a loveless contract, and she was a dazzling, brown statue standing at the crossroads of my paths. I followed her like a magician who, with his eyes fixed on a shooting star, allows his feet to take the first turn in the road. On a train to Kent, her kiss smoothed my fledgling lips. It was the summer of 1895, she was my first kiss and I was the first man she'd been with since her marriage. Olivia reminded me of my love, a distant glow, an invisible ideal that connected her to Maud. For no matter what I said or did, no matter

87

how much I looked into the distance, at the horizon where new, pink storms were ready to break, I could only make out the divine curve of Maud's face before the setting sun. Her copper hair was laid out across the sky; her face was pierced by grey, rainy eyes; she was the white flower that foretells the apple on the tree – Maud inhabited the sky, I could only submit to her on my knees.

While Olivia was still there, a regular visitor to my little apartment, Maud reappeared, like a divine ghost, between the stones on my balcony. She wrote to me. She told me that she saw us both among the stars, that we were travelling over the fishing village of Howth, that we were haunting the crenellated towers of Sir Edwin Lutyens's castle. We hovered, horizontally, hand in hand in the gardens, over the prickly hedges, in the beech alley or the rhododendron fields. I clung to Maud's arm as if it were the mane of a winged horse that was hurtling through the sky, leaping from cloud to cloud, crushing the lightning with its tireless hooves. She ran off without warning and flew alone to Paris. I fell back into the void. Into Olivia's arms.

12

It is nearly ten o'clock when Jacques Diallo finishes answering questions. Before going back to work, the Scattered stay for a while to decide what to do next. So much has happened since Madeleine called them together, since they decided to act as a group on behalf of their dead. They have swept the city from top to bottom, as amateur detectives, they have checked the most minor details with the institutions, the *mairie* and the funeral homes. They have combed the archives in the libraries; they have asked about Ireland, a country they knew only through the images that appear on their screens, the black lakes, the grey horses of Connemara, the wild plains dotted with standing stones. They questioned their painfully mute families, probed attic trunks, collected period photographs, death certificates that were crinkled with tears and yellowed by the years. They have gathered all the information that Roquebrune could provide on this affair.

Madeleine says that it is time to act, that the deception has gone on long enough, that it is time to obtain a court order for the exhumation of the remains, the DNA analyses, the unmistakable evidence. In order for each dead person to return to his or her own country, his or her own grave, they must go to Ireland, to take legal action and to have Yeats's grave opened. The lawyer is categorical on this point: only Ireland can decide to unravel the mystery, to discover who has been keeping the poet company in the kingdom of stones for more than half a century. It is time to leave, to prepare for the journey and to defend their cause. The Scattered nod in agreement, they are behind her. They vote to choose which of them will go. They vote for the war of the ashes.

William

Let's talk about my return, about heads in peaked hats hurrying past my brand-new coffin whose red wood – perhaps mahogany – had retained the majesty of the tree. What else had it retained? The remnants of a poet? The remnants of a Nobel laureate? Or a clever Franco-Gaelic mixture? The issue is still unclear and so scandalous that I am beside myself – my mind is outside and has no body to enter; my mind is left to itself, left to who knows whom. Rage makes my entrails boil – they have been soiled by profaning hands, soiled by earth which, because it was not right, it was not my earth and it has turned into a greasy, fetid, heady clay, freighted with anger of the betrayed dead. Yet I had taken the trouble to make my final wishes known; I had taken up my pen to say what had to be done so that my soul could take flight and find its next shape. My wishes had been dictated by the voice of the sages around Mareotic Lake, they had been recorded in my verses, relayed by the recitations of a thousand schoolchildren – I was to return to the spits of land in the country of my childhood, to be buried under the foot of Ben Bulben, six feet below my mountain. That was to be the final act. My chosen décor was the winter dawn that cracks the swollen wood, covered in a shroud of steaming ice. The air was as sharp as the tip of the sword of the horsemen who had emerged from the shadows, illuminating the fleeting night with their golden helmets. The brave were cast out, with a hissing, menacing breath, by the very mountain that had given birth to them. They rode on the tear-drenched ground, their pale faces devoid of blood and their bare feet sinking into the sides of their mad mounts. There were also those women with supernatural shapes, gigantic creatures capable of raising their faces above the trees, spreading their long, red hair over the highest branches, resting their chins on the treetops and singing the song of the dead. On the lower branches were statuettes of granite cherubs that the fairies had left as decoys, replacing the human babies they had carried off to be their mothers. The heavy statuettes were tossed about by the headwinds that blew around the mountain, and occasionally one of them would fall out of the nest and crack like an egg against the icy ground – a sign that the child would not return. My vision of the final act was a graveyard of dreams, a shadow ball where the birds of the day and night, the roosters and the crows, were fighting. In its wake, death always left roots in which the blood of past defeats and glories flowed, ready to blossom again in the spring, to take up the story where it had left off.

Who scattered the bones and swept away the souls? Who spat on the dead and their innocent neighbours? Who dared to perjure themselves on the interred poet? There is no greater misfortune than a bad death and an uneasy burial – someone who has passed away but cannot pass on. Their sleep turns to eternal insomnia, giving the ghosts puffy eyes under their sheets and feeding their thirst for truth. The ill-slept spectres shake like cotton wool in the tornado and keep busy by looking down from on high. Waiting for what? Only God knows.

The coffin sent back to Ireland, which remains covered by a veil for a while longer, was as robust as a log, gracefully covered with a marquetry offering me, the dead man, the elegance of the dandy. The splendid object was adorned with a gold plate on which my full name could be read. The coffin was blessed by the hands of the highest priests, the bones were purified by the grains of sumptuous censers. What were they guilty of, those exhumed remains of man, those survivors of the darkness? Does the body retain sin in its bosom long after death? Ten years passed in the shelter of the earth before the cruise was undertaken. Not without difficulty. The souls had to deign to emerge from the limbo in which they had taken up residence, to which they had grown accustomed through their long sojourn there. So who had taken care to coax the Cerberus, to put the hound of hell to sleep? The affair must have involved long negotiations. Like Orpheus, who managed to move Persephone, the companion of the God of the Dead, and convince her to free Eurydice, someone had certainly been responsible for pleading their cause.

What I can say for the moment is that the odyssey began with a great spectacle. The smoke of the incense awakened the Most High to keep an eye on the journey. In front of soldiers standing to attention, the merchandise was lifted by the ropes pulled taut by sailors to the heavy warship, a corvette that was more than three hundred feet long and had to ensure the return of the national treasure. From my cloud, what I saw above all were the red pom-poms, the eternally white caps and the torsos clad in striped tops, bringing back the humble remains, just as the officers of the *Belle Poule* once brought back Napoleon's ashes. Did the sailors, those frenetic gamblers, know that the dice were loaded?

13

The Scattered got up in the middle of the night to catch their flight to Dublin. The steward's slightly comical show after take-off put them in a great mood. Everyone is now enjoying the breakfast offered by the airline, an *Irish breakfast* of sausage, potatoes and white beans drowned in a slightly sweet tomato sauce. With her noise-cancelling headphones on, Madeleine sips the weak coffee served to her by the young man in the green suit as she watches the grey clouds swell through the window. On the other side of the aisle, the cobbler grunts with his mouth full, says he 'hates waste' and finishes the bean-pole's tray. The latter is delighted that his tabletop is free and takes the opportunity to fish out a book, a biography devoted to the poet; he sinks back in his chair and, despite himself, touches the arm of his neighbour, a smiling Irishman with icy-blue eyes and salt-and-pepper hair. The man is wearing a short-sleeved polo shirt and is not at all afraid of the breeze the air-conditioning spews out insistently onto the passengers. He glances at the book the beanpole is holding in his hands, a large volume with a brown cover.

So you're reading a book about Yeats? It's funny, when he got married he lived down the road from me, near Galway, in a tower, did you know that? I'm talking about Yeats in the second half of his life, when he was already a mature man, so maybe you're not there yet with your reading? Is it a biography you're reading?

Yes, he lived near Gort in County Galway, out in the countryside. My father also had his land there, he was a farmer – he's no longer with us now. I still live there with my family, my mother lives next door – she helps out with the kids. There are advantages to staying close to your starting point, you know, not moving too far away from your birthplace. Don't you think?

At one point in his life, Yeats bought a tower to live in, called Thoor Ballylee. Apparently, it was his attic near God, the window that allowed him to see what was going on above – if you know what I mean. When I was a schoolboy, I wrote an essay on the place. I saw it as a castle, a den, a magical place surrounded by stones. I was brought up on Celtic legends, you know, we're always telling stories here. W.B. – sorry, we always call him by his initials here – W.B. I imagined at his table, like a sorcerer in front of his books of spells, looking for incantatory formulas, making them dance on his tongue, declaiming them in his strange voice. I heard a recording of him reciting a poem; he rolled the 'r's like the peasant he was not, 'I will arise and go now, and go to Innisfree.' It stuck with me, and I remember that often when I used to walk in the Seven Woods, near my home, the poem I had learned by heart at school would go round in my head as if I was possessed. It drove me crazy, I could hear W.B.'s voice shaking as if he was going to burst into tears, as if he was going to die from his own words – I can't tell you what it did to me – his voice stayed in my head like a mouse in its trap, I couldn't get rid of it, every time I walked through the woods along the river and beside the lake he would come back to me and recite his poems. He always reappeared at the Seven Woods in those places that had inspired him so much, where he had heard the pigeons thunder, 'the unavailing outcries and the old bitterness' – do you know it? No? Heartbreaking poems. When I learned them – we had to learn them at school, you can imagine, as he'd written them near home – it almost drove me mad. Completely mad.

When I was a child we always talked about spirits in my area, spirits that took on unlikely forms; my grandmother said, for example, that her old neighbour's spirit came back as a steam-iron, that's saying something. You'll think I'm as mad as a hatter, but when I visited his tower – you know Thoor Ballylee? – I felt Yeats's spirit immediately, I mean physically. When I crossed his threshold, his spirit passed over my face – I'm not joking – I felt a load of hot, stinging, pain-ridden air. Do you know what happened to me next? It was as if I were suddenly under a shower of stones, invisible stones, ghost stones that poured down on me, like a real landslide on my skull. I thought I would crack. And then suddenly it was gone again. I didn't know what to make of it. But I'm keeping you from reading, aren't I? I'm too talkative, sorry.

Are you sure? Well, after that there was a change of scenery and light. Everything was pink, from floor to ceiling.

The whole room was filled with a sublime mist, you can't imagine how beautiful that cloud was. I started to hear something – you know, things go through my head a lot – this time it was a bird singing, so beautifully that I thought I had died, that I had gone to the other world. The mist, on the other hand, was moving, it was alive, it was moving like an animal. I got up, I wanted to follow it, to go in the direction it was pointing to. Its pastel smoke was everywhere, embellishing everything, creeping into all the gaps, twisting around the dusty chandeliers, hugging the shelves, lighting up the pictures on the walls as it passed – I remember the portrait of a sleeping baby curled up under a blanket. I think it was W.B. drawn when he was a child by his father. Beautiful as a star in the mist. The birdsong came closer, a few feet, a few inches, and then it stuck close to my ear. The bird wasn't whistling, it was reciting – reciting lines from a poem. Yes, it was reciting like a guy in a pub going off on a rant. The bird was even, I would say, a real storyteller, it carried the sun and the moon – I guess you know the poem – 'in a golden cup and a silver bag'. Well, you see, I didn't know it at the time, and the bird taught me.

What are you going to do in Ireland? Will you visit Yeats's grave?

*

The beanpole's mind is elsewhere, he is allowing himself be lulled by the cooing English of the man with whom he is sitting shoulder to shoulder. What exactly is he saying? Is he talking about a legend, or a memory? He's not sure he's grasped all the details of the tower talk, the story of the mist and the Yeats bird. Is there another madman waiting for him on his trip? He has a certain ability to attract them, a bit like sticky flypaper and flies. An innate talent. He feels them coming to pounce on him like the pox on minor clergy, like poverty on the poor world. All he has to do is to show up in his jeans and tormented, bewildered, exalted people come out like devils. The problem with this attraction is that it is mutual. He pleases the madmen who please him in return. He always falls head over heels for macho males, sensitive souls and undiagnosed schizophrenics who at the first whiff see Jesus in Eve's outfit fornicating with angels. Guys on the verge of being locked up, having escaped only by the luckiest of circumstances. He may know it, but he can't do anything about it.

The beanpole feels his armrest quiver. When the bare-armed Irishman asked him about his journey, he didn't answer immediately; he hesitated for a long time before revealing the event that drove the Scattered to meet their destiny, flying to the rescue of their ancestors. When he finally makes up his mind, his neighbour has fallen asleep, and the clouds in the porthole form a trompe l'œil pillow behind his head. The beanpole gazes for a while at the beauty of this milky figure, pale as death, and falls asleep in turn, lulled by the steady breath of half-open lips. He hears the warm voice of the prompter, its sensitive inflections in continuous streams. He speaks *of desolate multitudes, of the paleness of the moon, of a star that has come to light the wedding feast*. He sees what is said, what the voice recounts. A lion is gently dozing, no longer cold, *the whole savannah is snowing in peace*. In this white landscape grows a strange flower, with an upright stem, a blue rosebud covering the blooming life. Suddenly, hands from the depths lift the blanket of snow. The earth is bare, transparent, becomes ice. The tall stallion ventures out onto the hard ground, looks between his feet, discovers in the bowels of the earth, which have become visible, men who move. They are sewn together by their cheeks, their hair braided with that of their neighbours, they form a human flock. Their mouths speak inaudible words, muffled by the thick layer. He begins to smash the ice floe, hitting it so hard that his hands fall away from his arms. His body is shaken by a chill. In his sleep, the Irishman has put his hand as big as a bear's paw on him to protect him – the abandonment makes it even heavier. The beanpole remembers his dream. But he is sure he did not sleep.

William

As a young poet, I admired the refinement of my companion Wilde, the most accomplished storyteller of our time; with his silk-lined briefcase, his cleverly fitted furs and his knotted patent shoes, he waved his golden cane in the face of London society. No poet ever combined work and spontaneity as he did. Wilde dressed the world in perfect phrases and wrapped it in bright, transparent, yet lacy sheets. Wilde turned his life into theatre, his family into his most original work – his most beautiful facade.

As a successful playwright, Wilde competed with Shaw on the stage. He was the toast of London, with his hair curled like Nero, proud as a peacock displaying its tail of feathers; he was like a boxer showing his fists to a crowd of spectators. He made ostentation his supreme art, his sublime weapon. As a soldier, he would have been the greatest general; as a lord, he would have stuck Queen Victoria under her throne or sat her on his knee. Wilde's audacity engendered the wrath of the men of bad morals who saw in his abundant tenderness the reflection of their fears. Wilde loved and loved to talk of his loves. He stirred up the wrath of the shameful, closeted Londoners – and also that of Lord Queensberry, who called him a 'sodomite' – and lost both his temper and Queensberry's pretty-boy son. Wilde attacked the lord like a grey wolf pursuing a fox or a jackrabbit. He succumbed to the temptation of overbearing confidence and was dragged before the court at his own greatest risk, at his own greatest peril. Wilde did not run away from the island – did not set sail, did not go down the Thames. He did not borrow an inflatable to escape danger, to escape from the England that was working to ruin him. Wilde's only vice was his suffocating trial. His conviction, and later his death, were the first tragedies of the new century, and they paved the way for all the others. They made of the great stag a wounded goat, of the dandy a martyr. Lady Wilde, his beloved mother, had spoken these prophetic words to her son, the words of a mother as cruel as they were loving: 'If you go to prison, you will always be my son, my affection for you will not be diminished, but I will not speak to you again.' The Wilde family died one after the other; they never looked back, not his brother, nor his poet mother, nor Constance, his shamed wife. Wilde paid for the dishonour he had thrown in the face of the English, paid for it in his grave. He had a sixth-class funeral, the last before the mass grave. We had to wait for the resurrection of the sphinx, the winged poet and the author of *Portrait*. Thank God, it came.

Today Oscar has become king of the ghosts, forever my comrade. We are both leaning on the poets' balcony, on a cloud of rhymes, a cloud born from the rings of his cigar smoke. We are companions in dreams with our floppy neckties, looking down on the world below. Oscar says that it was made by fools for the wise to live in, that from here you can see its absurd layout. The mountains are bare, the hills bald; the stunted trees have witch's fingers, in the past, they seemed to reach for the heavens and flew away with the howling of dogs. The countryside has shrunk and has become so distant to us. We contemplate it like the forbidden city, above which we dance, like cursed chimaeras, with our dragon wings. I see the beginning of the hunt below me, the hounds awakened at dawn, running like insects along the bloody trail. They sniff the inert bodies of those who, dying in the mud, no longer feel the sting of the bushes, who no longer shiver from the cold of the earth. The dogs surround their prey for the kill; they suck the blood from the wounds to soften them, they enjoy smelling the scent of the still-warm meat and will soon sink their teeth into it. My eyes turn from the execution, that final scene. Oscar attracts my attention, pulls my chin with his gloved hand and shows me the proud mountain with its steaming grey flanks. The stone there is hollow as an egg; it is the tomb of our fathers, the last shelter where they drink and play their violins. 'What have they done with you?' my ghostly brother says. 'Go back to where you came from. Look closely at the road that leads to Sligo, to your land. Leave, William. Leave in search of yourself.'

14

The Scattered enjoyed just one night in the capital, one night in Dublin, before continuing their journey to Yeats country. A taxi takes them to Connolly Station, the station named after a dead signatory of the 1916 Proclamation, James Connolly. The chequered floor clatters under Madeleine's heels as she leads her small group that is running late. The beanpole rushes to the ticket machine; it spits out tickets to Sligo – one way, no return, they don't know when they'll be back. They go to the wrong platform and ask a porter for help; they run and get on the green train at the last minute, heading for another world. A voice calls out the names of the stops in Irish; they are unsure of everything, unsure about Sligo and about what awaits them at the foot of the mountain, at Yeats's grave.

It is nine o'clock in the morning. To their left, teenagers are disembowelling a giant packet of salt-and-vinegar crisps, which they munch and drown in energy drinks. No matter their age, the passengers are barely there – like ghosts, their heads are immersed in flickering screens, absorbing everything. There are no whispered words, no small talk between friends; the only noises that intrude are those that accidentally escape from the telephones, shrill, electronic voices, voices from beyond the grave. Outside the window, the city fades, giving way to the wild and dark countryside unfamiliar to Madeleine and the Scattered. Here, the white sheep wear masks, have black heads and legs, and horns. They are lying down – a sign that it is going to rain – stretched out in the soft grass, regularly sprinkled by the sky; long strands of grass dot their matted coats. A few kilometres further on, a herd of cows scatter, each choosing a different direction, each moving away to enjoy a few minutes of silence and solitude before moving into the barn. A dragonfly bird with its fringe-like wings flies past the carriage window, behind it the fluorescent coats of cyclists who, like the sun, cast their yellow light onto the forest paths. The clouds are so low that they seem to touch the earth, putting white caps on the tops of the mountains. Rough gusts from the angry sky whip the fields, the tufts of long straw, the young branches of the dancing trees, painfully following the cadence imposed by the wind, that rough rider. The austere plain seems to undulate joyfully, as if the spirits were giving an invisible party there, facing the sea reflected in the window opposite, which looks at them jumping each wave. Madeleine did not think this landscape would be as devastatingly beautiful: this forest of thin, blue trees growing as straight as leeks, populated by free, vanished souls jostling one another. They have left a wheelbarrow at the foot of a low stone wall nibbled by moss; they will come back later, under cover of the night for protection.

The beanpole deciphers the names of the stations that scroll across the electronic strip above the carriage, pronounced by the voice on the train: Collooney, Dromod, Boyle, Ballymote. Then it will be Sligo: the 'i' vibrates and the 'o' is closed. The journey also happens in language – the countryside has an accent. Madeleine's mind is racing along outside the window. *A land of giants*, she says to herself. *I haven't seen a man under six feet tall, and if I meet one, he will be an elf.* On the other hand, some trees are so small that they must be the homes of mythological creatures, concealing a tiny door opening onto a cosy, comfortable den. The matriarchal fairies are also from around here, moving from one world to another, from the wonderful land of youth and abundance to the land of men, going back and forth. Madeleine senses they are hidden in the countryside, in a hare's burrow, under a sheep's belly or in the petals of a butterfly flower. A couple is walking along the railway line, wearing windbreakers, with bare calves – it is sixteen degrees, the temperature of the sea, and for them, the weather is still beautiful – white, transparent skin and orange-blond hair, at thirty years old their hair is already going white. Madeleine tells herself that it is the clouds that discolour people's heads, she has seen Yeats's in a photo, his hair was as silver as the sinuous lakes that lie before, carving twisted branches into the landscape.

When they arrive on Sunday, nothing is open. Sligo is deserted, so they will have to improvise. Luckily the weather has remained dry, so they will certainly be able to see Ben Bulben, the mountain Yeats spoke so much about, under which he planned to lie forever. Their own deaths made no decisions. Their fate was left to chance. Chance took advantage of them. Great advantage.

William

In search of myself, I contemplate the sky around me and come face to face with my worst memories. Dark, poisonous spots, cirrus clouds full of rain and ice crystals, ready to pour down at the least disturbance, at the slightest wind tugging at their cloudy feathers. Maud refused me three times, granted me a few lost nights and refused the rest, made me fall apart. Iseult, her daughter, pushed me away in her turn. She had survived everything, the darkness of the dead brother to whom she owed her birth, the wrath and abuse of her dead stepfather, yet she gave up the place with me that her mother had left her. She did not take the sceptre that I held out to her, did not enter the kingdom of roses that my heart opened to her, my double love, for her and for Maud. She made her decision and the sword suspended by a fragile hair fell on my head – beautiful Iseult did not want me for a husband, she chose me for a father.

As a rejected lover, deprived of mother and daughter, it seemed to me that Shiva himself was slapping my face with all of his hands, with all of the fingers that denied the wedding ring, that the god's eyes were ready to close, to imprison the universe and me with it. Shiva's closed eyelids were, I learned later, a good omen. They announced the end of a cycle, the conclusion perhaps of my failed love affair. I didn't know how to get out of it, how to extract myself from the hole where I was playing dead, where I was amongst them, sunk up to my neck in the clay, with my legs and trunk planted among the roots, where only my spirit could still move. I could see the seven-league-booted thighs of the Irish messengers, the buckled shoes of the women, their Victorian slippers flapping on the surface. As I slipped down inch by inch, and my mouth already half-full of earth, my nostrils blowing only a trickle of air, the wind blew a reed out of the steaming swamp. I clung to the branch, to Georgie, whom Ezra Pound had introduced to me, the bohemian girl, the young, wild goose who, pulling Aphrodite's chariot, saved me from the depths into which I had been sinking for half a century.

To become her husband, the old husband of a young woman, took me some time. At the time of the wedding, I was still poisoned with unhappiness and my heart was tired of having chased others for so long in vain, exhausted by the burden of love I had carried through the storms. I wrote that evening, in the light of my honeymoon, regretting my love for Iseult and for Maud. I wrote, tossed by the contrary winds that made my mad soul as fragile as a cuckoo's nest. I wrote. I abandoned Georgie, who did not take offence, who wisely waited for the following nights, waited for my soul to be released, for her witch's spell to act on me. It worked a week later. Georgie also began to write, to put down in automatic writing what was being said through her, what the spirits were dictating to her.

'With birds, all is well in the heart. Your action was the right one for both of us, but in London you despised its meaning. You will have no regrets or remorse, and I certainly think I never will either.'

I cannot explain the relief that was mine, the ills that these few words cured as soon as they were written. The pain and the rheumatism were gone; the neuralgia was suddenly muted. No more suffering. An immense joy covered my sorrows, I flew as happy as a lark, like a bird spared by the hunter's bullet, discovering that life was still mine, intoxicated at the idea of living for the first time as if this were a new life. Georgie's flesh and mine, inflamed by the messages of the spirits, their oracles, married at once, to enjoy the divine excitement that tied our bodies to all the others, to all the beings that the earth had once borne. Shiva's closed eyes were the best of omens, the universe had taken a turn, had slit its thigh to give birth to a new world. My wife was a medium, she had a thousand new eyes to give her visions to the poet. So that he could procreate.

15

They walk down Sligo's main street, their eyes fixed on the murals that cover the walls, that invade the alleys, the cul-de-sacs, that span the River Garavogue, that line the footbridges – giant murals bearing the effigies of Yeats and Maud, the country's pride and joy, now a tourist attraction. On one of the facades Maud is gigantic, her hair done up in a high bun with a few locks falling down on her nape; she is dressed in black, with a ribbon around her neck. A story comes to Madeleine's ears, like an ancient tale travelling up the memory lane of Sligo to reach her. On the wall Maud is dressed like a widow, mourning her hero, John MacBride, who was executed by English bullets; she is pursued by the fire of the bloody Easter uprising that in 1916 fell on Ireland and its insurgents. The widow mourns the soldier for independence and forgets the violent husband, the abusive father-in-law. Death has made a saint of the drunkard, a martyr of the devil. Madeleine and her two companions can now see W.B. Yeats painted in profile, the wind turning his long, white locks into the wild mane of a snow lion. Behind his glasses, his eyes are looking into the distance, no doubt at the mountain whose crested slope forms a smile. Unless perhaps he is already looking, at the sunset of his life, behind her, in the other world. The poet and his muse are everywhere, spectres in their own country, their presence-absence hovering over the Scattered.

They go deeper into the city and discover the quays of Sligo and the Harp Tavern, an old pub with a black front and gold lettering. They wonder if the place is old enough to have hosted Yeats. Perhaps Yeats was a young man who came to take advantage of a stay with his grandparents to learn about the pub and declaim his first verses. This is an unlikely hypothesis; even though he is everywhere in the town, a proper brand name – *Hotel Spa Yeats Country, four stars for the poet* – at the Harp Tavern there is no trace of him. Instead, photos of traditional musicians line the brick walls, right up to the beams. They sit with pints of ale, a fiddle or flute in their hands, singing the timeless ballads 'Whiskey in the Jar' or 'The Irish Rover'. A painted plate keeps them company, a Celtic warrior occupies the centre, his torso naked, an eagle perches on his shoulder; he clutches a sword in his left hand, ready to defend the mountain of his ancestors.

Yeats is nowhere to be seen; yet, like him, the tavern is from another century, housing vaporous creatures as decoys. The scruffy-haired waitress has a chubby, dirty face like those of the farm women who once wiped their sweat with one sleeve and their brats' noses with the other, women who barely lifted their dresses to piss upright before going back to their tasks. At each of her words, her creamy lips curl up like those of a horse being harnessed. She looks at the Scattered with a look as empty as the bubbles that rise up the sides of the beer glasses and then goes back to the bar. Madeleine realizes that the two of them are the only women in the old pub, populated by sports-mad men as white as sheets who, hankering for sport, crowd around the noisy screen.

When lunch is over, the beanpole flags down a taxi and asks if it could take them to the foot of the mountain, to Drumcliff Cemetery where the poet is buried. On the windscreen a sticker reads: Jimmy Martin, seventy-two years old, a photo highlights the colour of the driver's hair and eyes, as grey as the sky. His singsong accent echoes that of the rest of the town.

'Well, it's quite a long way if you have to walk, nearly five miles.'

On foot it is a long way, almost eight kilometres. Yeats is buried in the graveyard at St Columba's Church, near the river. Of course, he is. I'll take you there.

*

Jimmy Martin, taxi driver

Yes, I'm from here, well from the countryside around here, but I know nothing about Celtic legends. To me, they're just old maids' nonsense, sort of witches' tales. I've always hated the stories about fairies, elves and whatnot.

No, again, sorry to disappoint you, but I don't know anything about Yeats and I don't want to know anything about him. I only know that he was a poet and that's enough for me. I pick up tourists outside the hotel or the tavern and take them to Drumcliff Cemetery, to the foot of his grave, full stop. The rest, well. The only thing I can show you, if you like, is his statue. You pass it on your way out of town, it's on the corner of Stephen Street and Markievicz Road. Ah, I warn you, you will not be disappointed. Look on the left, ah! Poor guy, they made a right mess of him – between the long-legged fly legs, his tight trousers and the pointy boots … A real lord. Not to mention his jacket full of poems. People say that it gives him wings. Mind you, you could say that he flew away. In his own way.

William

Here is the little party arriving at Drumcliff. They have followed
the road lined with wild grass, lined with red grass, have
followed my mountain with their eyes as it offers itself to the
winds. They know nothing of the danger; they know nothing
of Ben Bulben, the schizophrenic mountain, the grandeur
that raises it up and the darkness that inhabits it. They have
not seen the north face, the steep face of the mountain and
its toothy mouth of sharpened flints that swallows from this
side what it spits out in its heights, that kills in order to better
reanimate, arrogates to itself a godlike pleasure. To the north,
Ben Bulben takes the rifle from the visitor's hands, points it
and asks the wind to pull the trigger. Once finished, it readies
him like a rabbit, slits his flanks, removes his pyjamas of skin
and hair and swallows him whole. If the man is disarmed, the
mountain itself splits its limestone, its black shale, stretches
and becomes deformed, steep and slippery, an infernal slope.

They took the road to Drumcliff, to the cemetery where they say I am. They have seen only the gentle slope that carries the walker along like a mother, the slope that pushes the walker's soles to the flat top of the earth, that plunges his eyes into the bog and the tormented ocean, into the waves that cut violently into the coast. Its beauty is so striking that it revives the most desiccated soul, the being who is most lost, the one who while they lived liked to play with death. The mountain pushes that walker, pulls him by the collar, draws him to its peak, guides his finger to the divine border, to the edge of the other world, and makes him go back and forth. On the southern slope, Ben Bulben creates miracles, reconciles man with eternity and with his existence, with those that precede him and those that come after him, and gives the spirit a random form. The mountain revives everything and distributes the roles: for so many bodies, so many souls. The knight's carcass inherits the thoughts of the peasant, the father's thoughts inhabit the substance of the son, his arms, his hands that he knew when he was so small, that have perished from an unknown disease and now place themselves at his service. At the top of Ben Bulben, man lives and dies ceaselessly, he is eternally starting again.

Since the sky opened up, letting me fly in the windy corridors, letting my cloud approach the mountain, caressing Ben Bulben's head, I have been sailing between both sides. On the side of the dreams, I see my country of bushes and ferns, my almost-naked country whose sprigs and round leaves like lyres cover the legends. It was once the hunting ground of the Fianna, the warriors who served the King of Ireland, led by one whose hair, whitened in the prime of life, reflected his purity and grandeur. Finn's story sweeps through the land, oozes and rises; it is the Celtic sap, the blood of Ireland. Finn was a canny strategist and became the leader of the Fianna after many adventures. Because no king speaks before a druid, Finn was initiated into their art and became a master of speech and worship. He had been able to direct his father's weapons against the fire-breathing enemy Aillil, and had even placed the magic spear on his forehead to pierce it more easily. Finn had become the most far-sighted leader in the Celtic kingdom. The story goes that he dipped his thumb in the broth of the salmon of knowledge, where tender, pink flesh had been soaking, and he ingested all the knowledge of the world from the fish. Legends praise the fortitude of the indomitable giant whose epics are still told from Scotland to Ireland, somewhere among the clouds.

Leaning over the other side, I am caressed by the hundred-year-old trees, the bell tower of Columba's church and the thousand-year-old crosses on the graves. On the path slippery with yew needles and beech leaves, a bat that escaped from hell has stopped flying. It lies on its back, its dark wings outstretched, showing a surprisingly pale, evil face, its flat mouth open to reveal vampire fangs, foaming with its own blood. At the edge of Drumcliff Cemetery, the trees bend over to drink from the fast-flowing river that carries away their lowest, weariest branches, and drowns them in its bed.

16

The taxi drops them off at the cemetery gates. On the left, a small path leads down along the Drumcliff river, lined with trees that bow to them, smelling of earth and wet leaves. Before going to Yeats's grave, the Scattered decide to take the path and walk in the woods, to follow the river in the direction of the current. The path is narrow, so narrow that it looks like a pedestrian track, yet a car coming from behind nearly mows them down. Before crossing a makeshift bridge, Madeleine takes a photo of the yellow sign that hangs on the fence, advising the visitor to beware of the bull with ringed black nostrils. The silhouettes of the three members of the Scattered turn around instinctively. No animal is in sight. The coast is clear.

The river is high and flowing fast and dementedly; the noisy water overflows the banks, makes the earth muddy and weighs down the feet of the Scattered, which become mucky and dirty.

Soon they abandon the bucolic stroll in the footsteps of the poet, with their steps in his, they turn away and recoil from the giant puddles and the natural world that hinders them. They turn back, head for the sacred place that has drawn them here – the world of stones that the living build for the dead, to shelter them or perhaps just to show what remains of their presence, testifying to their absence. The stones say that they are eternal like the rock but are nothing compared to it – not much at all. They enter the small Celtic cemetery. Ben Bulben is so close, just beyond the wall that surrounds the dead; it seems to be a border with the other world. The mountain is so close that the graves seem to lie at its foot, like old, grey toes hardened by the years. The mountain watches over its dead and protects them from the wind and storms, sings stories to them that it knows by heart, stories which have traversed its walls, pierced its rocky skin, shattered its entrails. The immense mountain broods under layers of dust and empty carcasses, it feeds its green hair with them and above it hosts a great ball for the ghosts. The mountain is the great guardian to which Yeats's immortal epitaph inclines: *Under Ben Bulben.*

Like the seagulls around them, the three members of the Scattered now circle the graves to find the right one. They are almost all the same – they form humble pools of gravel, dug right into the earth. Here there are no frills, no marble; the cemetery is coloured in a palette of greys on which a flower bleeds red from time to time. Names and dates are engraved without any fancy effects, without gilding, without medals or photos. Identical graves for the identical dead.

Madeleine spots a couple of tourists in green waterproofs taking a photo; she waves to the others. This must be it. The alleged tomb of the poet, a stone's throw from the round tower and the old Celtic cross. On the thousand-year-old cross the roots of the tree of knowledge climb; they turn, twist, grow leaves encircling Adam and Eve, and the unwinding serpent. Above the original couple, parents of all the others, Daniel is represented with the famous lion who did not devour him. The biblical story says that Daniel, a blameless man, was given to be slaughtered for having been faithful to his god, that he was thrown into the pit at nightfall and that his god sent the angel to his rescue to close the mouth of the hungry beast. The Celtic cross pays homage to Daniel and to Christ in his glory who, by his side, day by day is fading away; he has lost his cross and is gradually being encased in stone like a shell, becoming a haloed ghost, yet another in a cemetery already teeming with them.

By the foot of a woman, an American tourist who teaches English and who has unbridled admiration for Yeats – she has studied his poems, his prose, his theatre – and to the left of the grave when facing it, lies a discreet stone. *W.B. YEATS*, not one word more, no need to distinguish him from the others, to specify who he was or what he did; those who kneel at his grave do not arrive there by chance. He himself guides them there.

The beanpole questions the tourist, her husband has remained a few steps away: does she know that the poet is probably not in his grave? Does she know that there are doubts about the cargo brought back from France? That in this affair no dead person is in the right place, that the dead and their souls are up in a heap, that the bodies have been dispersed? The sixty-year-old tourist gives him a polite smile.

She doesn't understand a word he says, knows nothing of the Scattered and their ancestors, and obviously does not wish to know anything about them. She had simply come to see what she had read, to see if Sligo lived up to the reputation the poet has given it. She has come to see what he set in stone in his poem. She looks at the land around her, the land caught between the sea and the mountains, she hears verses echo for everything, for Lough Gill, the radiant lake, the lake of legends that houses the island of Innisfree where the poet longed for peace, for the music of crickets, for the flapping of linnets' wings. The island is now inaccessible, unattainable, existing only in Yeats's words, as a mirage glimpsed from the shore, from Slish Wood, the fairy wood, or Dooney Rock. The American tourist does not believe a single word of the Frenchman's speech. He is crying wolf, rambling about corpse-stealing, imitations and the disappearance of the poet. Yeats is everywhere, everywhere she looks, on the backs of white birds, in the golden apples of the sun, in the torn sea. Suddenly, a voice, an inner voice like that of a narrator when she is reading for herself, reminds her of a story written by Yeats, the story of the man who dreams of Fairyland: 'This man found no peace in the grave.' A premonitory line? Did the mystical poet know beforehand that he would not find rest, that the earth would not give him the tenderness and care he had hoped for? Was he, who had chosen the exact location – the cemetery, the mountain and the river, he who Sligo calls its own child – stopped at who knows what border? Has the earth of France taken everything, sucked everything in, drunk his body, captured his dreams, blurred his visions? Do the poet's verses now revolve around his bones? She reads the famous epitaph on the tombstone, the troubled epitaph that sounds like a warning to the reader who has become a walker, a cemetery visitor, a ghost hunter.

'Cast a cold eye on life, on death. Horseman pass by.'

The American tourist and lover of Yeats goes up to the beanpole who, trying to crack the secret of the stones, is photographing the tomb, centimetre by centimetre. She walks towards him, the Cassandra-like oracle who may have told the truth, in whose mouth Apollo may have spat so that he would never be believed, never be listened to. She is tempted to talk to him, to ask him about the mystery he has mentioned. Then she changes her mind. What's the point of stirring up the dust? She has seen what she wanted to see; she joins her husband a few metres away, standing in front of the porch, ready to enter the church. The shadows of the cobbler and the beanpole saunter after her like ghosts.

*

Standing alone in front of the grave, Madeleine hears a slight buzzing sound. She looks for the insect, examines the rare wildflowers that push their way through the weeds. No yellow-and-black hairy shapes, no short and fragile transparent wings, nothing explains this muffled rustling, this humming that nevertheless intensifies in her head, that makes the tombstone vibrate and crack. Worriedly, she turns back, worried, to the desolate cemetery, abandoned by the visitors for a while in favour of the little church. They now wander through its nave, admiring the coloured stained-glass windows. Madeleine, on the other hand, has remained in the old, grey cemetery where a thick mist suddenly rises, settles on the graves, forms a white screen on which figures appear. On the carpet of mist, the Yeats couple lies sleeping. Georgie's short hair is messy; she is dressed in a light nightgown on which hangs a long, double-row necklace; her face is stern in sleep. A sepulchral voice, as if escaping from the depths, tells of her love affair with Yeats, a love of a new kind, a friendship held together by close spiritual ties, smooth as the surface of a pond. She tells of their occult alliance, of what the poet owes to the wisdom she allowed him to glimpse. Georgie lies on her back with her arms crossed over her forehead in a restless sleep. A sudden chill makes her shudder and gives her goosebumps. Her muscles stiffen, and her head shakes; she meets an instructor, a friendly spirit who honours her with his presence. Here she is whispering, intoning enigmatic words. The spirit speaks through her slumbering mouth:

'Creation does not flow in the right direction, there are no borders, no forbidden spaces, no neutral spaces, everything is complicit. Everything is in the one, the unity is total. What leads us astray is the multiple ...'

She gets up drowsily and sits down at her table. Everything is black, it is night. With one gesture Georgie opens the curtain, revealing an infinite starry field behind her. The poet is still in bed; awakened by the crash of the sky that has opened under his wife's hand, he gets up to join her. A milky way is now taking shape in the firmament, a glittering road dotted with cobblestones on which the poet, standing, is about to leap. Standing beside Georgie, so frail and small he looks like a bear walking on its hind legs, a bear with a lion's head, his pale mane floating before him in the new space. From above, other unheard voices bounce and overlap as he timidly ventures onto the celestial path. These are not stars but masks that dot the vault, masks that the poet picks up on his way, which he wears as he goes. Georgie continues to write, her head back and her eyelids closed; she is like a canal accepting that water that flows from her mouth, that pours out and waters the divine path with its light. The mouths of the spirits also take shape in the mist, the mouths of the instructors, twirling around Georgie who writes their sacred words. The spirits are unknown writers who breathe into her ears and direct her dancing pen; they curl the letters between her fingers like strands of hair. In a trance, she holds the ink-wet pen in her limp hand, lets herself go, lets the wandering souls enter her and spill out. She is the receptive force; she herself is a blank sheet of paper on which the names of Thomas de Dolowicz, Ameritus and the others write without control. They come to her, like Ulysses in Penelope's dreams, they come to put down on the page puzzles of words, fragments left as an offering to the poet. Georgie writes the scattered thoughts that the visionary spirits have drawn from the universal source, the common source, the great memory of the world. The words traced come from all eras, they are strikingly deep; they make visions grow before the poet's eyes, daisies tenderly shaken by a peaceful autumn, the inside of an egg appearing on the outside. The ecstasy that escapes from Georgie now forges whirlwinds, virtuous spirals that move her closer to her husband, that carry Yeats away and perch him atop an old tower. He sits like a bird of prey on a branch, contemplating and reciting the formulas of the spirits, the unreadable formulas written by Georgie, which he struggles to read. From the top of his tower, he addresses the instructors, the invisible spirits, conversing with them. His questions to them stretch threads in the sky, over which he jumps higher and higher. The poet ascends again and again, overcoming, surmounting obstacles. In the distance, he hears the hoot of an owl, the tinkle of a bell, the notes of a flute, the sounds of insects and the garden. He breathes in the spices, the scent of violets, roses and incense. He finally experiences the universe in its full and complete form. In this new state of mind, he finds everything that he knows, everything that he has accumulated, everything that he has seen in the previous lives that he has completed in order to be reborn, to complete his twenty-eight phases just like his star, the moon. The poet is reincarnated in his tower, the bear becomes a fawn, the lion a hawk, and then a man again. He is a poet once again; yet, stockier and more robust, poetry no longer oozes from his wounded entrails, it flows joyfully from his forehead like the dew on fine days. At his feet is the copper cauldron in which he has mixed, on the advice of the sages, symbols, crosses, cubes and geometric shapes; he mixes them and stirs them with his palm in one single direction, makes a uniform paste so that his poetry and prose sprinkled with truth can rise.

Suddenly, he swerves; a black spot has infiltrated the dough. Georgie alerts him with her mouth wide open, she writes that he should beware, that a spirit has lied, that he is not what he claims to be, that this clever spirit has come to frustrate the poet, to lose him, to mislead him. The poet removes the black pebble from the back of his spatula, he has been warned in time, he resumes his work and lights the fire. From the vapours of the cauldron foamy bubbles burst forth, images come to life. Nine and fifty brilliant swans fly out to the rhythm of their flapping wings. The swans, who thought they were prisoners of the lake, discover with wonder that, pushed by the wind, they have flown away and now make broken rings in the sky. Under the enchanted gaze of their creator.

*

The small clutch of visitors leave the church as if after a service. The Scattered find Madeleine, who dares not speak of the vision she has had of the Yeats couple writing together, hand in hand, creating in unison with the spirits. She fears that the poet's story has gone to her head, that it has permanently affected her. She does not ask the forbidden question – *have they seen it too?* It is an unmentionable question, forever unanswerable, suspended over her head like the canopy of a tree. Once again, the cemetery is peaceful; the sky, emptied of its ghosts, turns red and slowly darkens. Soon the light fades and disappears behind the mountain where Diarmuid, son of the sun god, once died, his heart pierced by a boar's tusk. As the American tourist couple set off on their wild journey, the Scattered leave the cemetery. Madeleine's mouth is sealed, still shaken by the apparition. She thinks of her dead child, of her lost aunt, of the betrayed child perhaps buried here under her feet. She must learn more. Go back on the road. Resume the investigation.

At the cemetery gate, the souvenir shop sells bits of the poet, mugs with his image, coasters and placemats alongside sweets for tourists, snacks to recover from the graveyard visit. In the window are some of Yeats's verses and a collection of jewellery with their motifs – a crescent necklace for the moon wave, for the ancient dances, hands and eyes mingled until the clear night sets; earrings to make the child dance in the wind, to shelter him from the roar of the waves; a gushing waterfall on a silver chain for the hills of Glencar. Still other images engraved on metal rings, bracelets, pendants for the webs of paradise, for the wine of love and for hands white as pearl.

The muffled atmosphere of the shop gently rouses Madeleine from her stupor. She spots a boy and a girl, friendly-looking lovebirds, certainly local. She asks them where to find a bus to the city, back to Sligo. The young man has tender eyes and freckled cheeks, he hears in the 'r's that clear her throat, in her accent, that she has come from afar, that she and her friends are worried, confused in the middle of the fading, darkening plain, amidst the graves and the night birds that are starting their celebration. He glances at the others, at the cobbler who is feeling the tips of the shamrock-decorated knives in the shop with his index finger, at the beanpole who is desperately dialling numbers that ring out and fall into the Sunday-night void of the dead town. He offers to drive them back to Sligo himself, to the station, turns to his girlfriend who remains silent, watching the Scattered settle comfortably into the seats in the van while her generous companion offers her a space in the back. Sitting on the paint cans, she holds back her anger, holds onto the headrests of the seat that cut her off from the others, that cut her off from the conversation taking place. It is about Yeats – in Sligo, as everywhere else in Ireland, it is always about Yeats. Here, writers prostrate themselves before him, flogging themselves, praying to God to one day raise them to his level; even musicians put his words in their guitar songs, in their piano melodies, between the strings of their harps. Since childhood she has heard them sing his allegories, heard the poet's fables; they sing of the aviator in the clouds above, the lost children who go hand in hand with the fairies, they sing the song of Wandering Aengus. In the pubs of the crows, the ferret, at the tavern of the fleur-de-lys, on Friday evenings you need only wait an hour or two for the cats to crawl before the full moon, and an old man, a fisherman, will raise his glass and with a loud voice recite what is left in his heart. The old man recites Yeats's prophecy, which he makes his own, releases the tears trapped in his eyes, on the edge of the abyss. Yeats's poetry gives him release, it says what he could not say himself, tells others that they are mistaken in thinking that he is nothing, that it is with the years that man improves, when exhausted by his dreams he can finally meditate and congratulate himself for having withstood the adverse weather. Yeats gives his countrymen his words, helping them to withstand mountains of sadness, he becomes a poet in the place of others, in their service, present on all lips; Yeats embraces them forever.

At the back of the van, her gaze is level with the bushes, she could trim them and prune their sides. If it were summer, she could eat their blackberries with her eyes and melt their black pearls in her pupils. In winter, night falls so quickly on the countryside; her eyes blink, sweep the shivering bushes like windscreen wipers. She grew up in the country and she knows that the bushes are not empty, that they are indeed inhabited, that men share their land with the beings below and that the acres of land here have been divided vertically. Yeats knew this too, he himself saw a fairy through his childhood window: he heard his mother, Susan, say that a banshee screamed when his three-year-old brother died, when the poet's brother left. The evening twilight awakens invisible forms, backs adorned with wings, veils, hair as long as dresses that mingle with the branches of trees; frail creatures hang from the leaves like caterpillars, curl around their stems, their cries join the wind that brings them to men. Yeats knew that the Sligo country-side was full of ghosts – the ghosts of the woods, the ghosts of the mountains, especially Drumcliff and the Rosses where the ground is dusted with their light footprints. The footprints of the weasel Ness, virgin warrior, mother of King Conchobar, meet those of Ossian's mother, transformed into a hind by a druid. Also on the soil of the plain are traces of the red dung beetle that gnawed at King Nuada's flanks. In these places, the past comes out at dusk, more present than ever, nothing separates it from the world, from the tourists who have come to wander along the poet's path. She knows that every tree, every stump they come across, is a passageway to the ancient times they believe are over, which still exist in the rock cavities, in the undergrowth, in the underground burrows, whose ceilings are lined with heather roots. Soon the rays of light will unbutton the black night, opening up its charcoal shirt. The streetlights illuminate the city, which is more deserted than ever, and the station. The van comes to a stop at their destination; the Scattered get out. The Sligo night swallows them. Swallows them up in one bite.

17

The sea around Dublin is so calm today, so tranquil that it inspires absolute confidence. It would almost be easy to forget that it is as cold and as icy as a gravedigger's back. Yet every day, every morning, as the feverish sun struggles to begin its ascent, breathless at the very start of its climb, bathers rush into the sea with their dogs as if it were a warm broth. In the coves along the bay, just in front of the houses of the lucky few who take their pleasure from many sources, who luxuriate in their proximity to both the sea and the capital city, men drop their trousers without modesty, revealing round bellies, thighs like flies and skinny buttocks, which they wrap in unflattering togs, to jump from the top of the rocks. The oldest amongst them throw themselves off the ladder with the bravado of a suicidal man, with the ardour of one who has chosen his end, for whom the ultimate pain is a real pleasure, and whom the sea will soon embrace. The women with caps are by far the most numerous, there are a few strands here and there that escape from the latex or the fabric, falling down over their eyes, protecting them from the spray and the sun's rays. They move forward with a sure step until the water arrives at the middle of their bikini line, in the middle of their belly, then they slow down, discreetly peel off the nylon from their breasts, curse the sky for these excrescences, for having imposed on them the nourishing organs which, in these circumstances, turn against them. Nevertheless, these women of all ages, and of all shapes and sizes, dive in and merge with the Irish Sea, into the arms of the stern nurse who welcomes them and shakes them to make them react, putting their bodies and their ideas back in place. It is said that the cold sea has magical powers, that it is the ultimate cure, that it keeps the doctor away and that it pushes death away with its waves. Unless one of the treacherous, murderous waves makes a tacit agreement with death – one drowned person for each moon; one body sacrificed for the others, for the ordinary bathers. The latter get off lightly, splashing around happily like wild ducks. Despite the season, despite the biting wind that chafes their fragile skin – in derisory comparison to the seals around them, with their glossy leather pelts – no one backs away, no one turns down the invigorating treat, the simple happiness within reach of all islanders.

The Scattered follow the seaside promenade, the path along Sandymount where the poet was born, they are on their way to the centre of Dublin. Jack, a member of the Yeats Society of Friends, is waiting for them on Merrion Street, where in Georgian times bulls and cows ran riot, where great fairs were held on the lawns, now a stone's throw from Dáil

Éireann and Seanad Éireann, the two Houses of Parliament of the Irish Free State. Yeats lived at number 82 Merrion Square, in a building owned by Maud Gonne, a brown brick building with sash windows between which his name is now inscribed on a bronze plaque. It commemorates the work of the great man, the writer, the playwright, the founder of the Abbey Theatre – Ireland's national theatre. Next to his name is always a comment, as if it were a trademark that accompanies, precedes and follows him: 'William Butler Yeats, the greatest modern poet in the English language' – as if no one else had a chance, as if he had taken everything. Yeats lived in Merrion Square between 1922 and 1928, having become father to Anne, Michael and the nation after independence. When Yeats was a senator, he made eloquent, historic speeches in favour of divorce and schools, and against censorship. He was the national poet, the first Nobel Prizewinner, a great man in the service of the emerging institutions.

Jack is in his fifties, good-looking, with an athletic frame and a greying blond goatee. He is waiting for the Scattered, who are due to arrive any minute on the next Luas. He waits in a tearoom in Merrion Square, on the corner of Fitzwilliam Street near the French embassy. For breakfast he has ruled out kidneys, beans and sausages, and chosen a place where everything is white: the walls, the chairs and the tables, everything except the cakes, whose cream is pink like the raspberries sprinkled with flakes, laid like miniature trophies on the oats. He and Madeleine have been corresponding by email for several months, discussing the enigma of Yeats's body. They have assembled their information, put together their ideas, and decided to join forces. Since the scandal, the Irish have looked the other way, as if nothing had happened, as if Yeats had returned safely home. However, by the time of the repatriation, the poet's friends already had their doubts, knew that the body had lain in the ossuary and even tried to dissuade the widow, Georgie, who wanted him back. At Yeats's second funeral in Sligo, the poet Louis MacNeice had seen the brand-new coffin on the shoulders of the sailors, had hidden his concern in black Irish humour and had said that a French clubfoot was inside. The Irish, too, suspect the assemblage of random remains, the bits of Frenchmen lying beside the poet's skull; they tacitly accept that they keep him company in the grave. They may not be the only ones in the coffin, as an Englishman wearing a corset is said to have unknowingly lent his back to the dead man, and to Yeats's supposed body, one or two others may form the arms, with others still supplying his legs. The hospitable Drumcliff burial ground is a place for many guests, a boarding house for the exiled dead, a mass grave in its turn. Some Irish people think that those erroneously repatriated at least enjoy charming surroundings, that they are side by side with the poet for eternity, that they would happily sign on the dotted line to take their place. Jack is not one of them. He makes no concessions about either the dead or Yeats; he knows his country like the back of his hand; he knows that in Ireland a rumour sets the world on fire, that it goes round the island in no time. Jack doesn't care. He refuses to accept the official lies. He's ready to help the Scattered, to raise the alarm and light the fuse. To raise the dead from their graves if need be.

*

It is a pleasure for me to finally meet you, dear Madeleine, to put a face to your name. Excuse me, hello to you too, gentlemen. Pleased to meet you, my friends.

Yes, I have consulted our archives, those of the Society of the Friends of Yeats, which contain every possible document, all the films in which he appears, the recordings of his voice, not to mention the writings, the work of researchers from all over the world. I have also interviewed Dan, the foremost expert among us, who has given me access to everything in the society's archives. This is all lovely, my friends, but it also hides the essential truth; it hides our internal divisions, our future civil wars. Some of my compatriots are firmly opposed to the opening of the grave, are ready to blockade it with their bodies to protect that of the poet. They see him as their father, as a saint; the weight of religious upbringing should not be underestimated, it is the most Irish atavism of all. No matter what you do, you always have a crucifix stuck in your brain, waving like the bell on an elf's cap. Inevitably, there are those who itch and fret – there's no avoiding it – who make themselves feel better by uttering bigoted nonsense, who say that exhumation is profanation and violation, that no truth warrants such sacrilege. You would think they were facing Tutankhamun, facing the onslaught of the vengeful mummy, you would think a curse was about to fall on the tomb-openers. If they are pious enough to believe in the soul, why are they clinging so tightly to a body? And why on earth are they so afraid of ghosts? It's hard to understand what's going on in those Irish heads, half of it is down to Catholicism, half to superstition. Heads always stuck in their legends, between two black cats and two pointed elf ears. They will do anything to avoid upsetting the ghost, to keep it well in its box, shut up with their fears. No, don't expect support from Yeats's Irish friends, they fear his return too much; they worship his memory. They will not help us. Won't raise a finger.

What I have to say to you, my friends, is that in Ireland everyone knows, everyone knows that the transferred body was just a symbol, that the coffin was filled in an unorthodox manner. It is an open secret. It is also known that the family turned a blind eye, tacitly giving their agreement to the minister of the time. How could it have been otherwise, my friends? How could they not have known, the family, the children of Yeats who were so close to the minister, who was almost their brother? I'm sure you know the story.

What? You don't know the story of the minister, the legend surrounding him? You don't know whose son he was? My friends, make yourselves comfortable, we will order another pot of tea.

*

The lips are moving, Jack Mulligan's lips in the middle of his grey beard with fine drops of Earl Grey clinging to it, and those of the beanpole translating his words for the cobbler's ears. This form of Chinese whispers communicates the two languages, portrays the minister and his relationship with the poet, before and after his death. The storyteller moves forward in stages, in the Irish manner, starting at the end, with the minister's prestigious career – he was a winner of the Nobel Peace Prize, a human-rights activist and a founder of Amnesty International. He gradually goes backwards, outlining the trajectory of the man who had studied in France, who had kept the music of that tongue in his language. The storyteller now imitates the minister's voice to amuse the French, replaces his 'th' with 'z', speaks with their accent, bursts their eardrums with his thunderous laugh. He does not, however, mock the admirable man, national tradition forbids him to do so, for the minister was the son of an Easter Rising insurgent who was executed with Pearse, Connolly, Plunkett in Kilmainham Gaol. The minister took part in the War of Independence, refused to allow his island to be cut in two, to be decapitated, and rejected the treaty with the English. During the Civil War, he fought against the Irish Free State and was imprisoned in Mountjoy Prison, the same prison that held the Frenchman Antonin Artaud for beating a Jesuit with his walking stick. But back to the minister, to his combat with the IRA, of which he was a leader before he opted for the ballot box.

In his armchair Jack becomes animated, moving towards the edge with each new revelation. He is all the characters to whom he gives life, to whom he lends his voice. He leaves out no detail of the great history of Ireland, of the struggle against the English who took everything, the land and the language. In his chair Jack is the revolution itself, the fight for independence, the Civil War, the statue that bears witness to the fighting, the sacrifices and the final victory. The Scattered find him delightful and enjoy sitting at his table, wondering what the end of the story will be, who the famous minister is. Madeleine almost forgets Yeats and his ghost, who flies for a moment through the terrace, whirls to the top of a majestic sycamore tree in Merrion Square and gazes down on the roofs of power. They remain seated, firmly planted in their plastic chairs, letting their cups cool, waiting for the next part of the tale, hanging on the grey lips. Jack finishes the sketch, the great historical parade, before placing the minister and the poet in it; he draws a large, black, feathered hat, the left side of which, when raised, reveals downy hair. Beneath the mourning hat appears an imposing, monumental widow whose curly hair swirls around her smooth face. Jack stands up for the final monologue.

'The minister was Seán MacBride, son of Maud Gonne and John the revolutionary, half-brother to the beautiful Iseult. He was a member of the family Yeats cherished all his life, the son he would have liked to have had with his muse. The minister went out of his way to bring the poet home, to please his mother and to bring back the lover of her youth.'

*

Madeleine can't believe her eyes or her ears and is astonished by this Maud who goes out the door and comes back in the window, who has been around Yeats all his life, even after his death, beyond him. It is as if there is always a thread to hang them together, to pull them towards each other, to put them back in the same basket. As if their faces were pinned together on a wizard's table. Madeleine wonders what happened when Maud slipped back, when she kicked the bucket, when she passed over to the other side. Did she run into her creator-lover again? Was her William there as she went over the hill?

Did she come smack up against the comfortable ghost, the one who had been waiting for her for fifteen years? Had he reserved a place for her, a place for the dead Maud, for the moment when she finally succumbed? Madeleine wondered if in this other life they had managed to do better, to make their love story a happy one, to turn the wheel in the other direction.

As for the minister, the intervention of Seán MacBride explained many things; he was the putative son, long desired by Yeats, his false father. He was the child whom the mother shared between two men, the drunken, valiant MacBride – the armed hero to whom he owed his body – and the thinker and poet Yeats, the inspiration for his mind. Again, this infernal, inescapable dichotomy that extends into unsuspected spheres, beyond what Madeleine had imagined, beyond what she could believe. The minister had drunk Yeats's poetry with his mother's milk, had listened to its background music as he sucked, had drunk every drop tinged with the mauve of the buds the Sligo spring brings to life along the reeds and black lakes. He was the child who had emerged from the shadows, from the fighting, bathed in the blood of the Easter Rising. He had washed himself in the clear stream that the poet had made flow from his pen so that a free island would be green, a new, changed island of terrible beauty. Seán MacBride was the worthy son of his two fathers: a warrior like one, a Nobel Prizewinner like the other. The two sides of the same Ireland.

18

Jack and the Scattered are driving towards the Society of the Friends of Yeats; the steering wheel is on the right, the car is thrown to the left, the wheels splashing in the puddles. When they arrive, archivist Dan O'Laoghaire is locked in his secret cell, watching a Super 8 amateur film in slow motion – one frame per second – checking its authenticity and its link to Yeats. To say hello, the two men wrap their arms around each other, pat each other on the shoulder and greet each other as they do here, chest to chest. Friends of friends are entitled to this too, landing in the archivist's warm arms, uncomfortably blushing, regaining their composure and concentrating on the screen.

Dan was given the film by a man named Alan, who had inherited it from his great-uncle. He had recently dug it out of the attic, had it digitized and then watched it, so discovering the truth. On the screen, the Scattered recognize the landscape, the flat-headed mountain; they see children sitting on the windowsills of houses, black sedans from another time, parked on the side of the road. One of the vehicles is longer than the others, it sits in the middle of the road, its bonnet strangely decorated with copper ribbons. Soldiers, helmets on their heads and rifles on their shoulders, are lined up in front of a high, grey stone wall that borders the entrance to a chapel. The Scattered absorb the compact crowd: women with headscarves carrying dark umbrellas, men in Sunday suits, hats in hand. They lay wreaths of flowers – green, white and orange – on the sparkling car, which is as long as a magpie's tail. They note the numerous members of the clergy (at least three Anglican-looking priests in black albs and stoles) who wait in the front row for the procession to pass slowly. Six middle-aged men carry a precious wooden coffin, wrapped in a vast shroud in the colours of Ireland; they pass through the silent crowd. The three French people in front of the screen witness Yeats's state funeral, the poet's return home, when the great man glides horizontally to his final resting place. The film is authentic, made by a jazz musician who happened to be in Sligo with his band on the day of the funeral. And who captured the ceremony with his camera.

*

Dan O'Laoghaire, archivist

At first I was very sceptical – most of the films sent to us about Yeats are copies of those we already have. We think we have everything, that we know everything about him, yet the French documents, the embassy documents, show that there are still grey areas, which are more important than we thought. They undermine of the attitudes adopted by our respective governments. In the Society of Friends of Yeats, right now, we are asking ourselves an ethical and philosophical question – what do we owe him, and what do we owe his memory? Is it appropriate to proclaim all truths loudly and clearly? I am not just talking about the fate of his body after his death – did you know that in his last days the poet was accompanied by his wife and his mistress? I am talking about Edith Shackleton Heald, the journalist, she was the last one, but not the only one. Before her there was Dolly Robinson, Margot Ruddock, Ethel Mannin. Not to mention the androgynous Dorothy Wellesley, the one who otherwise batted for the opposing team, so to speak. According to the poet, she went through life like a young man who also, and curiously, revealed the feminine side in him. This was when Yeats experienced a second youth, a second puberty, late in life. He had genuine feelings for his mistresses, but the physical details remain unknown.

It must be said that his mind was always overflowing with sensual energy, that as he grew older this desire became trapped in a sick body. He couldn't stand it; he flooded his poems with his unfulfilled appetites and lent them to his characters. *Crazy Jane* is a telling example: in the most daring language, she shouts to the world that old women have as much desire as young ones. Yeats was obsessed with the hourglass, with time passing, altering innocence and beauty – if there was any beauty there to begin with, of course. To return to the poet's ageing body, he rebelled against unjust nature, submitted like Freud to Eugen Steinach's rejuvenation operation, which aimed to restore his capacity as a lover. His poetry depended on it, he could no longer write because it was connected to the general ferment of his being, the engagement of the body that stimulated his mind, and was rooted in the smallest pleasures of the flesh. The poet knew this, he knew that he was writing under the impulse of lust and rage because of the fury that flowed like mud in his human veins, his lasciviousness, which he described as heroic. He had to regain his vigour at all costs. Let me assure you that the operation in question did not involve any monkey glands; it was, as we know today, a simple vasectomy, which Steinach thought at the time would revitalize him. Unfortunately, this did not happen.

Nevertheless, Yeats found subterfuges – ways of experiencing new emotions with these women that gave rise to poetic tremors. They did everything in their power to inspire him in his last hours, to keep him alive in the midst of the freezing winter that erupted in January 1939, even in Roquebrune. His last poems date from those moments, when he called his relatives and peers to his bedside, asking them to judge the poet's work and to prepare the old stone cross in Drumcliff Cemetery. Everything about him is incredibly intertwined, I tell you, body and mind are inextricable. When you know that, what can you say about this case? How can we not care about his remains, which are like the sap of his manuscripts, his final pages, and yet, like all of us, doomed to disappear? All of this makes my head spin. I don't know what to think about it, what he himself would think about it. What we do know is that Yeats, feeling he was on his way out, asked Georgie, his wife, to bury him in Roquebrune, to wait until the newspapers had forgotten him, before digging him up like a tree and replanting him in his Sligo soil. Those were his intentions.

As for the various opinions expressed by my compatriots on this subject, on the table is a file I have prepared for you. I will not make a decision in this painful case. I might as well cut off one of my arms. Or even both.

*

The dossier contains articles from all different periods of the case. Journalists were not the only Irish people to have investigated Yeats's death, to have wondered about the fate of the poet-senator, cornerstone of our independence, lifeblood of the Free State. Researchers, historians and biographers also resurrected the archives and letters and discovered that his wife, perhaps by mistake, had him buried in Roquebrune, in a vault intended for the poor. A vault that was emptied into a common grave by the war that Yeats had foreseen, and had predicted in his verses as a blood-blackened sea, in which even innocence would be drowned.

In the file, the Scattered find the articles they know by heart, plus Michael Yeats's strange request to have the bones measured before adding them to the coffin, as if he wanted to make sure they matched his father's build, the poet's height. They learn that the family of the English corset wearer Alfred Hollis, Yeats's neighbour in the grave, has been talking to the poet's family. Together they have abandoned the idea of DNA testing, for fear of awakening painful memories, of adding new pain, of being swallowed up by the chaos into which the father's physical death had thrown them.

In the lines deciphered by Madeleine and the Scattered with Jack's help, Yeats's death is compared to that of Shakespeare, whose skull was, according to legend, confiscated by grave robbers and whose remains also disappeared. Two deaths that do not sound like endings but generate mysterious after-effects, elevating the authors to the rank of gods, forever immortal. Too busy reading, Madeleine does not immediately smell the perfume emanating from the file, which, discreet as a church mouse, is now wafting around her in the archivist's small room, swaying as if it were a shadow of her figure and penetrating her nostrils. A clean smell of beard soap, of a clean-shaven face, of honeyed candle wax sprinkled with cologne, a smell that is moving, coming like a shooting star from the left, while to the right a completely different scent emerges – the odour of berries, of wilderness, the scents of Ireland wrapped in sacred fragrances, fragrances of incense. She sniffs her scarf, her jacket, her hands, unable to identify the source, she sniffs her loose hair. Realizing that she is the only one to notice it, she asks for the window to be opened. Outside, there is only the smell of salt water combined with the cries of birds, of the gulls that jeer, pursued by gulls that take the bread out of their mouths, that wound their already-red legs with their beaks. There is no trace of perfume outside the room, of the little cell that contains the tracks of the poet's past life, that holds the history of his body as a man who has lived and loved, who has experienced his poetry before writing it, who has allowed it to visit the smallest recesses within her, to take on the essence of his pleasures. The perfume bewitches her, carries her away, it is a journey into the poet's bed where warm exhalations, vapours of diaphanous skin, dripping with dew and desire, are stirring. She hears the whispering of women's voices, the sweet voices of the night that address the poet by his initials, guide him with their breath. He answers them with his deep voice, his full voice, a fearless voice that caresses those that whisper. He speaks without interruption, fills their bodies with visions, with a thousand hands that touch them, a thousand mouths that make them shudder, make them tremble like leaves. But he does not stop, speaks twice as fast, and pushes them to the limit with his fearsome words, his evil words that break down the last barrier, penetrating their skin without even touching them. He speaks, opens the doors with his voice, stands on the threshold, recites until he loses them and revels in the power of his words, the power of his rhymes over these women. They are now free, floating on the velvet, in the satiny intensity of the poet's country, the country he has woven with images, they incite him from the top of their heavenly spheres to join them. The poet, inspired by the sirens, climbs onto his canvas of ink, writes aphrodisiac words aloud, secretes magical exhalations that the muses in turn breathe into his mouth. The perfume concentrates, electrifies Madeleine's body, rises like a fire irradiating everything in its path. Suddenly it slips out of the window and vanishes, leaving her in the cell with her burning face, her cheeks red as fire irons under the bellows. Silence and torpor take hold of her again, take hold of Madeleine who doubts herself and her senses. Has she heard the enchanting, bewitching voices, the urgent murmurs, the rustling of breath? Has she entered the chamber of the poet and his muses, the fertile, inaccessible alcove from which rhymes miraculously emerge from the thrills? No one is present, by definition, at the preparation of the fire, at the scratching of the sulphur of the match against the rough box; there is no spectator for the first sparks, the first embers of the epiphanies that come to the poets, that give birth to their lines. Why did he invite her to this scene? Why did he choose her as his interlocutor? Is his mind playing with her to keep her from his path? Or is he trying, like the instructors in his time, to guide her? As Madeleine wonders about the messages delivered by the spirit, Jack tells the others about the cases of exhumations of famous people that have been debated in Ireland in the past. He has gone through them all with Dan and compared them to Yeats's case. He now knows how to do it. Jack is as stubborn as a mule. When he has an idea in his head, it doesn't go away.

19

Jack takes them back to Toner's, the oldest pub on Baggot Street, the most 'traditional', as he usually tells the tourists. When the poet returned to Dublin to embark on his career as a senator, his career as a public man, he had to experience, if only once, the pub he detested and whose bluster he shunned. Until then he had reserved his drunken moments for private functions, moments when he was safe from the onlookers and the barflies. When he arrived in Dublin, he convinced his friend Gogarty, also a poet, to help him fill the gap in his knowledge of the pub, to accompany him to Toner's, the door opposite, and to drink a little pick-me-up with him. Toner's is a cosy, welcoming pub, inside there is even a snug, a private space like a confessional, a hidden place to chat and drink without being seen, to sin in the discretion of the dark wooden walls while bathed in light through the large window. Yeats slipped in with Gogarty, ordered a sherry. He drank it down in one gulp, like a bullet on a deer's hide, and then proclaimed, 'I've seen what the pub is like, now take me home, please.' He got up and went back to his life as a senator.

Jack tells the story to Madeleine, the cobbler and the beanpole, all of whom sit in the snug as if on a pilgrimage, in the church pews that 'welcomed venerable posteriors'. He tells them that the Irish don't go to the pub just to drink, unlike the English, that they go mostly in the hope of getting a laugh, that 'in Yeats's snug', after a few drinks, the tone does not always correspond to poetry. The foam from Jack's pint washes his goatee, whitening it. He returns to the case and others like it; explains that Irish people are campaigning right now to bring Joyce's body back to Dublin, to his hometown; that this gives them food for thought, paves the way for Yeats's own funeral march. James Joyce is buried in Zurich; Dublin councillors have in recent days put forward a motion to have his body exhumed, to bring the author back to his city for eternity. The diplomatic process has begun; the battle of the bones is certainly fraught with difficulties, the city of Zurich wants to keep Joyce in its cemetery, but it is not certain that it will succeed. In Joyce's case, experts are debating whether he wants to be buried in Ireland, to return to a country he left of his own free will and to which he never returned, the island he called a sow after his exile. There is no ambiguity about Yeats's will, about the intentions that were engraved in his poetry; the battle that concerns him is a diplomatic one: where was the Nobel, mistakenly placed? Has a decoy been put in its place, like the fairies swap babies in legends? For what reason? To deceive the good, naive people? Jack finishes his beer, he's going to contact the members of Sligo Council, convince them to put forward a motion in turn. He will tell them about the Roquebrune Scattered, that the truth is due to them, that the Irish are not alone in this story. He writes a message, which he sends before their eyes. He promises on the heads of all the patron saints of Ireland – religious and pagan – that he will get an answer. That their request will not go unheeded.

*

While the others drink, Madeleine broods; she doesn't know how to tell them about this crazy idea that has sprouted in her skull like a bean in cotton wool growing long, tender shoots, taking up all available space, obstructing everything else. It is all she thinks about now, the spirit of W.B. Yeats sending her messages, an idea mixed with the fear that she does not have the right key, the right keys to open the doors that lead to her thoughts, to the convolutions of the ghost that has risen from its tomb. From Sligo, from the cemetery, it seems to her that the spirit of the poet has been following them as much as they themselves are pursuing him; that the hunt has been reversed, that on the now-blurred tracks their footsteps are intersecting. Are they walking, without realizing it, in the shoes of the ghost, waiting for him to lift them up with each step, to lead them to their goal, to follow his tracks? Or is he perching on one or other of their shoulders? Perhaps he has the power to slip directly into their bodies, he who is as free as the air which he no longer breathes, to slip into the form he has chosen and guide it from within. Madeleine would like to find a specialist, someone capable, like the poet's wife in the past, of getting in touch with the spirits, of recognizing the signs, of deciphering the messages. In a book on Yeats, she recalls a photo of a medium, Helena Blavatsky, whose circles he frequented, who communicated with the other side. A mysterious woman with scowling eyebrows, eyes that spilled out over her eyelids as if they wanted to come out of them, whose frizzy hair was hidden under a never-ending veil that was wrapped fifty times around her oversized face, her terri-fying figure. Madeleine has found her way in. She leaves the Scattered to chat in the snug and joins Jack at the counter. He is waiting for the next round of drinks he is buying his guests, she can finally talk to him, ask him what he knows about Helena Blavatsky, about the witch and her powers.

Jack launches into the story of the clairvoyant who was known as 'Madame', the prophetess who travelled the world, learning the rites of the greatest healers, shamans and mystics. He paints a portrait of the medium with clumsy fingers, whose rings made the rims of the teacups she read from vibrate, making them tremble as the ground trembles under the foot-steps of giants. Blavatsky came into contact with the dead and also with the spirits of invisible masters who sent messages in writing, raining letters across the floor onto the heads of those who questioned her. She was, in Yeats's time, the high priestess of occultism, of theosophy; she inspired artists and poets, gave birth to mysterious legends. It is said that she was capable of inexplicable feats, worthy of the greatest magi-cians, that she gave piano recitals without having learned music, that she knew how to speak all languages and how to write admirable verses in them at full speed. She was an outstanding hypnotist, so magnetic that she acted on her patient, on the spectators of the session and even on herself if she was not careful. 'Some,' he said, 'accused her of charlatanism. I can see how this might be perplexing, but I tend to trust Yeats, who knew a lot about this, describing witches floating on the mountainside, speaking in strange tongues, answered by angels and birds.'

Madeleine drinks in his words and feels inebriated by the witch-musician-poet's tale and by the first pint she swallows in one gulp. She continues to drink, keeping up with Jack's steady pace and his rising elbow. She no longer hesitates, takes advantage of the intimacy provided by the counter, fronts pressed against the zinc, taking advantage of the wait, the slow service and the general hubbub, to formulate her request. She does not mention the misty figure of the poet in the cemetery, nor the perfume of the muses in the secret room, she only asks if he knows a medium, a seer or 'a sort of witch'. She wants to get 'an idea of these occult experiences Yeats was involved with', she would prefer he didn't tell others, she has 'a personal matter to settle with the spirits, with her own dead'. Jack looks at her for a moment. He bows his head, does not answer. Instead, he opens his colossal white hands and shows the thick lines that snake across them.

'I've heard of an old lady who works upstairs at Parnell's Restaurant – a white witch, as they say – who reads the palms of customers, who is said to communicate with spirits. You'll find her easily. Everyone here knows her.'

*

Soon everyone goes home. Jack returns to his home, the ground floor of the house he rents in Ranelagh. When he arrives, his student daughter is on the phone, the light is on in her room, a trickle of voices is coming through the door. He sits in the living room, checks his messages, a Sligo councillor, Fiach O'Neill, has replied. He is, he writes, an admirer of Yeats, he knows the Society of his Friends, he is looking forward to talking to one of its Dublin members, he offers to call him tomorrow at three o'clock, if he is available. Jack responds with his big thumbs tapping the telephone keypad, accepts the politician's proposal and informs Madeleine immediately. He settles down at his desk, under the lamp that illuminates the shelves of old volumes, the chiselled and gilded spines of the poet's collections that he has been collecting since his adolescence. The books that surround him are like dear friends, familiar arms into which he can fall, which have held him a thousand times before. They saved him from the melancholy mountains, from the institution for boys in which he was imprisoned, that almost killed him. The churchmen, the abominable evening caresses, the muffled cries of pleasure on his back had so traumatized him, so wounded him that he had become dry as a heap of dead wood, ready to burn in the flames of the hell into which the priests had deliberately thrown him. As he was about to succumb, battered by the delirium that was turning into a creeping madness, he had been given a book of Yeats's poems as a gift. Jack had attacked it like a dog and read it as if it had been written for him, for his dying young mind, shattered in its fragile shell. He had swallowed the strength in its words, tasted the music of its verses, discovered a heart torn like his own. From then on, the poet had never stopped speaking to him with each new reading, each page, his words lined Jack's bed like a prayer, like salt keeping the demons at bay, the religious who felt he had become invincible. Yeats had guided him through the blind night, led him to the glittering moon, urged him to wallow in the green mountain grass, to take hope, to grasp life.

'Hi, Dad.' Like a cat, Jack's daughter pads across the living room to the kitchen, putting the kettle on for tea. Jack's fingers glide over the computer, making tiny sounds as he presses the keys, he prepares his speech and backs it up with verses, authentic evidence of Yeats's last wishes, clues and testimonies he has accumulated in the archivist's cell. He also gathers messages from Madeleine, elements that speak in favour of the Scattered, of the truth for which they have joined forces. He has plenty to do: he works all night, crafting his arguments, making them incisive enough, razor-sharp, as Yeats's speeches in the Senate once were. He thinks of the archives he listened to with Dan, of the rolling voice, the powerful tone of the Nobel laureate who knew how to make himself heard, how to hit the nail on the head in the midst of the din, beyond the tumult of the assembly, among his fellow men. He gathers the fragments from his memory, the hundreds of pages read, loved, recited by heart. All those bits of the poet that he has had vibrating in his guts for decades. He makes of Yeats a thick file for which he will plead the cause post-mortem, his own and that of the other dead.

Meanwhile, the taxi of the Scattered speeds across the Liffey, leaving behind, on its right, the huge bronze statue of the national hero, Daniel O'Connell, for whom the street is also named. It whizzes along the street, taking advantage of the off-peak evening hour when cars stand still like hounds in front of crowded restaurants and pubs. The driver drops them off in front of the hotel and takes off like a thief in the night. The tall cobbler and the beanpole don't want anything else; they totter upstairs and collapse into bed amidst the fug of Guinness on their breaths. Madeleine says goodnight, turns around and escapes without saying a word. Parnell's Restaurant is only a few minutes' walk away. The moon is bright and Madeleine tries her luck. At this hour, no white witch has yet gone to bed.

20

Madeleine leaves the hotel behind her, walks along the pavement, passing the Hugh Lane Gallery, whose frontage instantly reproduces her walking avatar on large electronic panels, like a shadow, a doppelganger following her. She passes a homeless woman with a crumpled face and missing teeth, a prematurely old lady with jeans that are too big for her, pushing a trolley in which she piles up her treasures, objects gleaned here and there from the rubbish bins: two-legged stools, pitted mirrors, broken radios from which she hopes to get a few euros, a few rocks for her pipe. In her high-pitched, feverish voice, she shouts at a poor bent man who hobbles along, scraping the ground with his leather shoes he drags around like slippers, the tops of which he has taped up to make them fit. Madeleine doesn't understand the woman, doesn't understand a word of her northside English, the syllables that spin around and are barely eaten by the damaged mouth that gave birth to them. The shrivelled man behind her can't hear anything either, can't hear his distressed companion who is bawling her eyes out and coughing at him. He mumbles into his tangled, yellowed beard, as if he were talking to an invisible person. *He too hears a spirit*, thinks Madeleine. She is not amused for long by this pun, does not smile at the hopeless words of the poor devils who together face the misfortunes of life on the street, the solitude in the middle of the world that makes them disappear behind the wisps of smoke they swallow, which they swallow at all hours to escape their suffering. One day, the intoxication that warms them and whispers in their ears, that keeps them going, will without doubt cause their death. What will they hear then? Will they be voices, spirits in their turn? Madeleine quickens her pace, puts a few metres between herself and the misery that has finally darkened her, that turns the cheerfulness of the beers shared with Jack into black vinegar. She looks up, reads the names painted on the facades; a window is lit up, that of Parnell's Restaurant which, 'Phew,' is still open.

Madeleine needs to recover before the meeting she dreads, she forgets her efforts, her resolutions, dines on a club sandwich at the counter. The soft bread is filled with a slice of bacon crushing the chicken, on which the cheddar melts, which rubs up against the tomatoes. The lettuce is bathed in an aioli sauce that leaks through the crack in the bread, spilling onto Madeleine's fingers, which she licks as discreetly as possible before dipping them into the plate of chips. She rinses it all off with a light lager this time, half a pint, just enough to give her the courage and strength to face the wooden spiral staircase and, at the end, the witch. The rates are posted on a sign next to her name: *Sally Fomorii, medium, €30 for reading the lines, €50 for a clairvoyance session and card reading.* Madeleine has booked her turn. She waits for the green light, which comes after a few minutes; the waiter points to the winding staircase, the waxed wooden banister that Madeleine grasps with her whole palm. She goes red from the heat of the climb, the after-effects of the alcohol, the emotion that rises with the rhythm of her upward treads; they mingle on her face. Her slow steps bring her closer to what attracts her, to what she has travelled hundreds of miles from home to search for in the Dublin night, which she nevertheless dreads facing alone. Yet here she is, upstairs, in the low-ceilinged, modest mezzanine, furnished with a bench for the medium, a chair for the client and a table with a white tablecloth from the restaurant, on which rest the tarot cards.

Wearing a black shawl, shrouded in grey hair that hangs down over the upper part of her body, Sally Fomorii turns towards her the opaline face of an old redhead; with her squinting green eyes that she closes after greeting her as if she could see better through her eyelids. She nonetheless welcomes her client with a half-moon smile and an air that testifies to the fact that she is not afraid of anything, that no misfortune can reach her, nothing can shake her from where she stands. As soon as the introductions are made, the hands shaken, the medium congratulates her on having chosen the clairvoyance session, which unlike reading the lines tends to make people run away, makes them afraid of seeing the devils inside them, which sleep within like never-extinguished volcanoes. Sally Fomorii finds the Irish as superstitious as nuns, resenting the fact that they fear a mere old crone like her, who is willing to help them find their answers. She is not what they say she is, not a witch, a restless shadow who casts curses, who interferes, who intervenes in the grand scheme of things. The medium explains to Madeleine the mystery of the gift she has been given, the rules that govern it – her ability is limited to seeing the future that is taking shape. Everything else escapes her and is played out in other dimensions. She speaks with emphasis, underscoring what she says with her hands, the entities that do her the honour of settling on her, who, like a parrot on a captain's shoulder, let her navigate, when the sea is calm, among the silhouettes sown by the fog. Sally Fomorii then briefly lives the lives of others, experiencing the movements, the shocks, the cracks and bumps that await them. She flies to the spheres that are familiar to her, in which she is used to immersing herself several times a day, in the company of the crowd of spirits who give her news – smells of oleander when it is good, of burning when it is bad. It is not a matter of magic but of webs, of threads that link men to each other, living and dead without distinction, linking them to the spirits who watch each other, spy on each other like hawks. They make it their duty to guide her, to find in her person – and in others – antennae, receivers, mouths to articulate in order to make themselves heard and play the role expected of them in the afterlife.

In her small practice, her wooden mezzanine, Sally Fomorii sees all kinds of people come and go, from the great and the good to the most popular, including psychoanalysts and what is left of the clergy. Politicians come to her in secret, asking her what will happen after the elections or about their problems with the British. They ask her questions but scarcely listen to her. For thousands of years, a curse has caused prophecies to fall unfailingly on the ears of the powerful and the deaf alike. When a tragedy is announced, a misfortune greater than that which affects their island or the world, they yawn, get bored, put their hands over their ears like schoolboys refusing to listen to reprimands. They ignore the threat that hovers beneath their windows and systematically gallop back along the road they have been advised to avoid. Sally Fomorii gives Madeleine the example of a minister who came to see her on Sunday evening, of the unease that gripped her when he entered. A weight radiated from her forehead and temples, accompanied by a terrible vision: deserted alleys, ghostly streets, people cloistered in buildings like Carmelites, children's cheeks pressed against the bars of the balconies where they were prisoners. A terrible evil, without any remedy, was going to fall upon them, was going to pick on the most fragile, was going to put them underground, was going to change the situation. She warned the minister, told him he had to be prepared for carnage, for thousands of sick people falling like flies, for bodies lined up, wrapped up in a hurry, for coffins piled up, for anger fed by tears. He did not believe her, did not feel the wind of the arrows that crossed his forehead, and underestimated the message delivered by a friendly entity. He left, sneering. *He will regret it.*

Sally Fomorii now asks Madeleine if she feels ready to listen, to hear what the presences have to say. Madeleine does not take much notice, she takes a deep breath, leaving a few seconds for excitement to overcome her fear. She nods silently, resolutely. With her eyes fully closed, Sally Fomorii begins to speak, in a voice that is not her own. At least that's the impression she gives to Madeleine, who lets herself be carried away by the flow of words from the clairvoyant who informs her, describing her visions in a thousand details. She opens her eyelids again, the green of the iris becomes impenetrable, like a sea of seaweed that stirs before Madeleine. The voice has sunk to the bottom, in a voice that could be male or female; it vibrates intensely in Madeleine. She asks her to listen carefully to the spirits, not to be satisfied with answers to the small questions of existence. To accept the missions entrusted to her.

*

Sally Fomorii, psychic

I am told that this is an arid period, which requires you to take stock, to remove the thorns, one by one, so that the bloody wounds cauterize, that you can in no way avoid this journey, this return to yourself, that the tensions have their source in the confused, poisoned waters of childhood. I am told that your quest requires both the prudence of the snake and that of the sheep faced with the wolf, that rigour is required in order not to be harmed, not to be betrayed, in order to overcome or bypass obstacles. I am told that during this sensitive, tormented period, vigilance is your armour and your shield against the devastating disappointments whose dust forms whirlwinds of sand and storms in the desert.

I am told to warn you, not to rush in like a bull; the new red cloak that presents itself wants to wrap you up, muzzle you like an animal. You must resist the urge to rush into a fight that takes you away from your target, away from your task. Follow your dreams, you can trust them absolutely, blindly. The mirages that pass through you are stars that imperceptibly guide you on the best path, they carry a golden cup on their backs, a sacred cup laden with fruit that you will taste when it is ripe.

I am told a very happy thing – a person emerges, someone who knows the steep path you have embarked upon, you will receive his help, I even see that he bends before you to give you a lift, to propel you to your highest point. This being is by your side all the time, he takes up your cause in the shadows, he gives you his powerful protection from on high. Thanks to him you will triumph over jealousies, internal wars, fratricides and all those who seek to block your way.

I am told that the victory is within; you will overcome the loneliness that blights your life. The message is a good omen, you can be sure of it. Nevertheless, the conditions outside are not ripe for the light to shine because the ray that lights your way does not come from the sun. It comes from the moon.

*

With these words, Sally Fomorii picks up the brown leather case on which there shines a sun with curved rays that dance like lightning. The case protects the tarot within it, which answers the client's questions, provides her with precise help and resolves dilemmas. The prophecy is still buzzing in Madeleine's ears, she concentrates nevertheless and tries to formulate her questions as well as possible, to proceed by stages, by concentric circles, starting from the centre and widening little by little. She asks if the dead child of her family is still in Roquebrune, buried near her family?

The long, thin fingers, whose wrinkles trace a hundred thousand lines on the fortune-teller's hands, as if so many lives were waiting for her, shuffle the deck nimbly and spread it out upside down on the table. The back of the cards creates an optical effect, it is strewn with tiny blue helices that plunge Madeleine into a second state, she sees in them the blades of a chopper, ready to turn, to stain the beautiful white tablecloth with the blood of the truths that are going to be revealed to her. The clairvoyant's right hand goes limp at their touch, letting go of the claw formed by her thumb and forefinger to catch the four cards, to form the cross of the draw. She lifts the left hand, a blue moon appears, diffusing its faint glow, the star weeps, its tears are licked by two dogs encircled by towers, at the foot of a pond that conceals a crab swimming vertically, claws extended. Sally Fomorii tells Madeleine that the women in her family, her elders, have been gagged, that they are counting on her to break the silence that suffocates them. The curtain of eyelids falls again on the green gaze, the cheeks tighten and deepen, Madeleine can no longer discern in the seer's face anything but a skull, a bare jaw speaking for the dead, telling the story of Jeanne's child, the secret of her grandmother.

It was not an accident, it was not a natural death that took the child ...

Madeleine sees Sally Fomorii's story come to life, scenes flash across the face of the seer whose translucent skin has become the theatre of her visions. She discovers Jeanne, barely out of her teens, as frail as a twig, a braid down the middle of the back of her flowery dress. She throws herself at her father's feet, begs him on her knees, with all her tears, repeats that the man from the ball loves her, that they will get married when he returns from military service, that they will make amends. She tries to extract the blood from the heart of stone, from the old tenant farmer with the curved moustache who growls, hears nothing, does not believe in the promises of the boy from a good family. He reminds her of the fate of unmarried mothers in the countryside, demands obedience. He will not take on the burden of the child left in the care of a nurse, will not bleed himself white for his unworthy daughter, his little idiot. He decides and orders the death of the unborn child. Jeanne's mother stands behind him, her features austere, her hair pulled back, separated by a parting in the middle of her skull. She looks like the Virgin, speaks in a subdued voice, repeats to Jeanne that she must obey her father and do what is necessary, that she will have other children later. Jeanne collapses on the cold tiles, one hand on her stomach, on the child she does not yet feel. She alone is judged guilty, the only victim of a life conceived by two, which risks costing her her own. Madeleine sees her praying for the man from the ball to come back soon, for a miracle to happen. Hope fades with the pressure of the days, of the winter which reinforces her doubts, causing the last leaves to fall. Soon she leaves the prison of the room, resigns herself to the torture, submits to the diktat of the father who despises her, spits on his wife and daughters who serve him, who address him as if he were a pope. Now Madeleine sees neighbours, women who are busy around the young woman's belly and giving her funeral recipes. Jeanne jumps ten times from the top of the stairs to unhook the occupant of her womb, allows herself to be poked with needles, her nightgown is wet with the blood from the hell she is suffering. But the baby does not come out, it thwarts the family's plans and clings to Jeanne who changes her mind and takes over. She finds the man from the ball and seals the promise. Fate reverses itself, finally turning in her favour. Madeleine is moved by Jeanne's revenge, and by the unexpected and finally happy marriage. The belly grows until the first snowfall and does not show the traces of the mutilations, of the wounds that have not disappeared. In the end, they get the better of the foetus. Death has taken over. It has caught up with them.

Shaken by sobs, Madeleine sheds tears that are hundreds of years old, those of Jeanne, of her martyred body, of her desires trampled beneath her father's boots, of the anger and mourning buried, drowned in the mass grave of misfortune. The seer returns from limbo, she slips through the last curtains of smoke, opens her eyes to Madeleine and gives her the answer to the cards.

The stillborn child is neither in Roquebrune nor in Sligo, her body is not in any cemetery. She has taken another path. Follow the spirit, you will find her.

21

Jack put on his black velvet jacket and thin, grey silk scarf, his walk slowed by the Oxford brogues that hug his huge feet. During the journey, he rehearsed the speech written for the councillor as if he was going to deliver it himself. On the train, he tuned his voice to the rhythm of the shaking, sharp, piercing notes of the rails that set the tone. Now he walks down John F. Kennedy Parade, strides down the riverbank, sees two early-morning joggers in the distance, hooded as if about to pull a heist. He passes trees bare from the cold of the season, bicoloured buildings, half granite, half brick – 'This country,' he says to himself, 'still divided.' He turns into the street that leads to the powerhouse, to the angular, columned building in which Councillor O'Neill is about to plead on their behalf, in which the fate of Yeats and the dead he dragged in his wake will be played out. The motion to be presented at 2 pm is addressed to the mayor of Sligo and the council's chief executive, and calls for 'all steps to be taken to clear up the matter of Yeats's grave, and for all the dead to be returned to their families'.

It's 10 am when Jack walks through the glass doors of the lobby and empties his pockets onto the scanner mat. The alarm at the gate sounds, he is asked to take off his belt, the damned shoes that cut into his heels and his watch with its steel bracelet. The circus lasts about ten minutes, Jack comes and goes, removing a layer with each trip. 'It's been a long time since anyone asked me to take my clothes off,' he says to the security men, who don't laugh, and run him through the detector and identify the metal, the St Christopher medal around his neck. Jack can finally enter. He goes down the stairs to join the team that has summoned him to put the final touches to the speech.

The Scattered have been busy too. From Dublin, from their hotel room, they have passed their documents on to Jack, the list of the dead buried near the poet. They are now talking over the hotel breakfast, between two slices of gluten-free bread and two spoonfuls of almond milk, porridge for the beanpole, two scrambled eggs with bacon for the cobbler. They have risen with enthusiasm, full of hope for Jack, for the speech and debate they will attend this afternoon in Sligo, which will be broadcast on national television. This morning the Irish press is full of headlines, radio and television have the name of the poet on their lips, the national hero may be exhumed. The role of the Scattered was also outlined in the columns; the rumour spread like crazy, it spread in the little capital of Ireland, it swelled like a tick. The Scattered were approached by journalists, Madeleine asked the beanpole to respond, to take the lead.

She was still tired from the night before and had told her team that she would stay in her room until she left for Sligo. She didn't set an alarm when she got home from Parnell's, she lay flat on her bed, allowing her eyes to close the moment her cheek hit the feathery pillow. She is still sleeping. Her eyelids are twitching. Jeanne is with her. She is as she has always known her, a grandmother with short silver hair, deep smile lines at the corners of her eyes and lips, and perfectly white false teeth. She waves her hand, calls her 'my darling' in her sweet voice. She offers to lie down beside her in the adjoining bed. Madeleine is happy to find her, happy to see her so well, she walks towards her barefoot on the wooden floor. With each step, a creak sounds, like a threat. Madeleine, worried now, tiptoes along, hoping to drown out the noise and anxiety within her, that won't stop in spite of everything. She follows the familiar voice, the grandmotherly voice that encourages her, that overcomes her fear of the creaks, which are getting louder and louder. She understands that they do not come from the floor she touches with her toes but from the bed she is approaching, which shrinks as she gets closer, which when she reaches it is no more than a child's nappy, a linen cocoon embroidered with her initials. 'My darling,' Jeanne repeats, lifting the sheet so that her granddaughter can slip into it. Madeleine seems to lose herself in the proportions of the bed, of her grandmother, smaller than ever, as thin as a fish, next to whom she feels like a colossal statue, an elephant capable of destroying without even realizing it, at the slightest mishap. Now there is a knock on the door, and in comes a man in a black shirt and a morning jacket over long flamingo legs. With a tray on his palm, he offers tea to the ladies, he has not forgotten the hour, pours the amber drink into a cup and hands it to Madeleine. She takes a few sips; the tea is sweetened with honey of the flavours of childhood: mountain, chestnut and lime. It eases her throat, tightened by her fear of making the bed collapse, and then the floor and her grandmother in its wake. She empties the cup, drinks the last drop, the furniture expands, the room widens, the walls push themselves up, the cot fits Madeleine's silhouette, who is stretched out across it. Peaceful. Her grandmother leans over her: *my darling, my daughter*.

*

It is almost 1.30 pm. Jack is polishing his prose, revising each word, weighing up the syllables, making sure it produces the right effect, the right sound for the adviser. In the same office, huddled around a meeting table, the team prepares their representative, feign untimely interruptions, provocative questioning of enemies, the emotion that will surely sweep the crowd away when it comes to answering for the dead. O'Neill must keep a cool head, must keep it on his strong shoulders, must serve the cause of the pillaged families, of the betrayed poet who had himself held office in his time, had known how to rise to the occasion, had fired up the masses with his speeches. The rifle is loaded, the bullets ready to burst from the barrel through the muzzle, to shoot towards the sky and its ghosts, towards the earth that has deceived its inhabitants, covered up the lie, been an accomplice to those who have taken the honours and spat on the graves.

Jack has finished writing. There is nothing left for him

to do but wait, to sit with the Scattered who have saved him a comfortable chair to watch the show – a front-row seat for the battle of the ashes. The chatter stops, the Speaker enters. He unrolls an interminable agenda, provides a post-prandial soundtrack for the councillors, who are mainly men, drowses them out with his monotonous voice, makes the heavy, grey heads droop onto ties and chests. As the words seem ready to extinguish themselves, to choke under the weight of their own weariness, O'Neill is finally given his say. He knows that he will have to roar to be heard after this, to split the silence and touch the spirits – Yeats's spirit is with him.

The councillor stands up, unfolds his lean, heron-like body, runs a hand through his thick hair. The fire makes his cheeks shine with sweat, produces a vapour that fogs up his glasses, clouds his gaze fixed on the room, which is silent and awaits the first words that are slow in coming. He clears his throat, puts his hands on the desk, takes a long time to arrange his papers upright. For the time being, no chin is raised, no eyelid opens, no deafened ear feels the imperative need to open up to what is still struggling to happen, to become reality. Only the families directly concerned are fidgeting in their seats; the cobbler and the beanpole are stamping their feet, casting sidelong glances at each other in which excitement gradually gives way to doubt and anxiety. Beside them, Jack is chanting, blowing out the first sentences of the speech he knows by heart, tapping the rhythm of the words with his big hands clapping his knees, hoping that the energy of his vibrations will reach the councillor, fortify his courage. Everyone is impatient, tensing up like bows, except for Madeleine, who as soon as she entered had smelled the freshly cut bouquet, recognized the flowery scent of roses, violets and the heralding mist. The smoke now zigzags over the stage, forms a soft cloud, draws a cotton halo that pours its rain on O'Neill. The icy shower washes away the chosen one's fear, rekindles in him a lion's passion, a fierceness he did not know he had.

*

Speech by Fiach O'Neill to Sligo District Council

Ladies and gentlemen,

I find myself today in the eminently sensitive position of one who shakes off the dust on which our feet have been resting for decades, who stirs up the ashes of the old fire of our independence, of our painful history, the ashes of our island's national treasure, William Butler Yeats, the greatest of poets. It is with his memory like a sturdy cane made from the wood of an ancestral oak from Sligo, his land, that I speak to you today. What have we done with his body, with his memory, with the great man who in his time boldly stood before the Senate in favour of freedom, of divorce? What have we done with him?

I am not one of those who believes in lies, even by omission, who believes in the virtues of state secrecy, in judicious silences. I believe that the truth is always at the bottom of the hourglass, that like a shell it eventually bursts, taking away those who have buried it to serve their mediocre interests. Here is a truth that was pushed underground and has come up to explode in our faces, that threatens to pierce our eyes if we remain blind to it.

As you know, there is great uncertainty about the identity of the remains supposedly belonging to W.B. Yeats, which our government brought back to Sligo after the war. An unbearable uncertainty which undermines the promise made to the poet of being returned to his homeland; it also undermines our own humanity in our dealings with the families from whom the dead were taken.

It is true that the error of this episode is not ours alone; we have proof that it is the fruit of shameful diplomatic arrangements, of deceptions wrapped up in the flags of France and Ireland, which are tied together in this scandal. Yet we have an opportunity to clear our consciences, to confront the sins of our fathers, to make amends. It is your duty and in your power to serve the truth, to exhume the grave which visitors from all over the world, travelling admirers of poetry, deceived by our inertia, betrayed by our indifference, have been visiting for over half a century. The time has come to put an end to the subterfuge that make us hypocrites and accomplices aligned with the perpetrators.

I can see your worried faces, your fears at the revelations that will come from the tomb. Fear not, no scientific analysis, no truth will take W.B. Yeats away from Ireland; nothing will tear the poet away from his nation, from the people he fought alongside. His work, his eternal poetry, is on the tips of our tongues and buried deep in our hearts. Fear not, the poet is immortal, his words live in our flesh, in our bones, his posterity is guaranteed, he is untouchable. Let us refuse to let make a mockery of his death, to allow it to become defiled, profaning thus his memory and ours. Let us take up his fight, let us make the poet's end the very embodiment of justice for the dead and their memory. Let us remember the innocent victims, the exiled dead and their families who are desperately searching for traces of them. Yeats's repose will be all the more peaceful for it ...

The counsellor is so engrossed in his subject, so filled with the memory of Yeats whose speeches, readings and public appearances he has read thanks to Jack, that right from the start of his speech he takes on an emphatic tone. Although he usually speaks too fast, his voice slows to sound slightly old fashioned, articulating each syllable, respecting the intonations of the text speaking with verve that must have lurked below the surface, just waiting to emerge, to fight a battle worthy of the name. O'Neill is possessed, even his face is transformed; with every word he utters his features lengthen, his nose narrows, his soft jaw hardens, his eyes seem to deepen like those of a hawk, they shine with the brilliance of the joust he is waging, going head to head with the council. He is on the side of the ghosts, adopting their supple gestures as if he were riding on their white backs, on their swan-like wings. Jack feels the emotion rising through his powerful frame, catches himself wiping stray tears from his full beard, small, salty lakes between two rough ears of corn. In O'Neill's rant, the wind that blew the ashes from the coasts of France to those of Ireland can be felt, the wind that pushed the dead from one ridge to the other. It returns to swirl over the island, starting a storm. No, those dead did not let themselves be pushed around; with Yeats in the lead, they went underground, flat on their backs, through the sticky basements of the common grave, the galleries of wars, the corridors of massacres where bones pile up in bundles, where humanity is reduced to dust. They had the strength to reach the stone, to open the trap door of the tomb, to demand justice. Those dead have done the impossible, they deserve the truth, they are nothing less than heroes.

As the speech ends, and the gauntlet of the demand for exhumation is flung down before Sligo Council in front of television cameras beaming the story around the country, the audience splits into two distinct, roughly equal groups, hermetically sealed from each other. On the right-hand side of the room, a herd of elected officials, surrounded by their staff and elderly constituents, remain unmoved, denying Councillor O'Neill any applause, making the crowded place buzz with disapproving whispers and low, disapproving murmurs. On the left, meanwhile, there is wild applause from the passionate crowd, making the walls tremble from the ground to the pale neon lights. Jack and the Scattered stand up, along with their neighbours, and a good half of the councillors follow suit, carried along by the movement of hope that has started by clapping hands and drumming feet against the wooden floor, as if to encourage the dead to show up too.

The Chairman returns to the podium, impassively resumes his role with the same soporific tone and confirms that the motion is passed. Before concluding, he announces to the room that the council will be sending a request for exhumation 'in proper order, to the relevant departments of government: the Department of Culture, the Department of the Gaeltacht, the Department of Foreign Affairs, the Department of Justice and of course the President of the Republic of Ireland'. The ball is in the court. On their side of the net.

They have managed to board the 7.38 pm train, see the land-scape go by in reverse, the stars bright, the path of light from the windows of the scattered farms, the moon plunging into the forest of shadows. Jack, the cobbler and the beanpole savour the first victory of their private war like soldiers. They replay the scene a hundred times, talk loudly, toast each other with their bottles of beer bought from the catering cart. Jack has freed his feet from the uncomfortable shoes, he puts his silk socks on the empty seat opposite, takes the crumpled speech out of the inside pocket of his jacket and shares it with the whole carriage. In his tenor voice, he rereads the best passages, punctuating them with his contagious, powerful laugh.

Madeleine does not take part in the festivities; she sits to one side, her nose glued to the window. Her eyes drown in the inky sky, in the darkness of the Sligo moor, they cling to the hundred-year-old trees, the speeding train making them tremble like poor old men. It all seems so far away now, so futile: the motion to ministers, to the president, lying some-where on the pile, probably underneath, tiny steps in the land of giants. It may take another century to resolve the matter, it may take an eternity for the light to shine on the dead, for its rays to destroy the secret, to cast out the shadows between the intertwined skeletons. The energy that carried Madeleine up to now has lost its strength, the passion has given way to a gentle, profound energy, opening a door to another setting in which the dead and nature are with her at all times. The shrubs, the bushes, the wild hedges are running after the speeding train at this very moment, she imagines seeing the curled-up fern fronds trotting along, the mushrooms jumping on their fibrous single foot, the daisies rolling on their corollas, the brambles crawling on their thousand thorns. Moss lies on the back of a hare, a crested cormorant on that of a horse galloping along the tracks; bats are on its tail, landing on the roof to make the journey. County Sligo follows her in a strange procession, escorting her into the night.

In the train, voices fade, mirroring the twilight, and stress gives way to fatigue and the calm of the evening. The long carriage is as deserted as a church; the ticket inspector has gone to his compartment, he undoes the first button of his shirt and pulls down his cap. In the carriages, eyelids come down like curtains at the end of the show, necks sway, deep breaths fog the windows, replying to the wind outside. The train carries passengers sleeping like children in its gigantic belly – two brothers here, head to head, over there the frame of a young woman half lying down, her handbag for a pillow, behind her an elderly couple whose hands are gradually being pulled apart by sleep. The beanpole's cheek bounces gently against the cobbler's shoulder, who himself shivers at each of Jack's bear-like snores.

Madeleine has also been mown down; the bewitching merry-go-round of the busy shadows has sucked her in without warning. The glass made cold by the ventilation escaping from the grate, makes her cheekbones red; she shivers. The high-pitched cry of a hawk pierces her eardrums, a clear sound that rings out in the silent night, like a call. The echo of the calling bird of prey comes closer, Madeleine straightens up, discerns two yellow eyes that illuminate the darkness, revealing the landscape of an old sea cemetery. The hawk lands on the large wall that surrounds it, scratches the stone with its beak, buries into a cavity it has arranged as a ledge lined with green – blades of grass, soft, padded leaves – in which lie three pale eggs speckled with red spots like a hundred eyes capable of seeing through the shell. Madeleine can make out the sound of three beaks struggling, of three young falcons breaching their shells. To free themselves like wise men.

Epilogue
Saint-Pancrace Cemetery, Roquebrune, 13 January 2016

Carlo parks his scooter near his premises, starts his rounds at the upper cemetery and goes down towards Saint-Pancrace, his body moves to the rhythm of his fingers pulling up the bits of wild grass. On each terraced landing he checks the state of the walls, the steps and the smallest cracks that could cause the stones to collapse, burying the dead a little more under their weight. He is the only caretaker of this hectare of dead people, of more than two thousand graves, of the human remains that lie scattered there. He sets to work at dawn, maintaining the two fields of rest that have been entrusted to him, which nature tenderly caresses with its branches. The work is colossal, Carlo's cemeteries – the new and the old – are surrounded by forests, by conifers which, in spring, spit out their pollen, their needles, their pine buds, pouring thousands of cones on the ground and testing his mettle.

Fortunately for him, he is as well-equipped as a horticulturist, a gardener and a nurseryman. He has a sixty-centimetre rake, quality hoes and picks and a broom for the leaves. For the flat plots, he has his hedge clippers, for the weeds that invade everything, that take advantage of the paupers' plots to carve out a space for themselves on the ground. Carlo clears every inch of his strange domain – he thinks of it as a huge dead person who contains all the others – cleans the in-between graves, in-between heads, in-between feet, the stairs too and the gardens of remembrance. He pulls up everything by hand, on his knees – weedkiller is forbidden – everything that is in the public domain, right down to the abyss of the old cemetery, right down to the sea that irrigates the tombs by their roots. Then he throws the remaining weeds into rubbish bags, which he carries on his back, bending under the weight like a Celtic harp.

Mornings, he attends the opening of the vaults, the bringing together of corpses, which must be completed before nine o'clock to spare the visitors from seeing what awaits them, and to protect them from a vision of the end. Nevertheless, it happens that some early risers come across corpses by accident; some of them can handle it, and they are even curious, but the legislation states that this is not desirable. When the vaults are opened there are sometimes unexpected results, such as when the coffins have deteriorated like the bodies, are pierced, collapsed one on top of the other and instead of eight corpses, there are now twelve. They are then left down below, just as they are, crushed, in a small common grave between relatives, under the new ones that the undertakers install on crossbars and a new floor. Everyone ends up in the pit at the bottom. Carlo supervises the work, checking that the remains are the right ones, the ones indicated on the application form.

After eleven o'clock he is at his desk in the old chapel, the one in which a painting once depicted a Christ with angels. It has also been damaged and could not be saved, unlike the statue of the Virgin Mary – a great survivor – which serves as his companion as he pores over his papers, constantly interrupted by families who call him, looking for their dead, by funeral companies who come to make engravings and ask him to consult his registers. Exhumations happen in the morning, burials in the afternoon; some days – it happens rarely – the two are done together, a space is made and immediately filled, an eternal cycle.

These days Carlo ends his day 'wrecked'; too many graves are abandoned, forgotten by relatives, some of whom have left town without informing the *mairie*. He takes it upon himself to fix the things that have fallen into disrepair, to do some housework. His job is to advise and maintain. He regrets that so many caretakers have become caretakers by default – 'as a punishment or a hiding place' – that some no longer do their job, that they only see the function as a sideline to their free accommodation, emptying it of its substance. He is an old-fashioned caretaker; he is the eyes and ears of the cemetery, he knows what goes on there. For example, he knows that one night a black mass was held in the military square, he found bowls with red candles and painted symbols behind the graves. The surveillance camera saw nothing, could not distinguish the strange ceremony, the silhouettes hidden in the darkness. Luckily, it only happened once, and the paint came off as if nothing had ever happened.

This morning, as his tour comes to an end, as he stands on the steps of the seaside cemetery, he hears strange flapping. Falcons, usually so placid and more faithful than any man, are having a cockfight. At least, that is how Carlo feels when he approaches and discovers the birds resting on the Yeats memorial that the strong gusts in the night have knocked off the wall. The stone lies upside down on the grey steps, the face of a winged unicorn pressed against the ground. When he arrived near them, Carlo noticed that it was not a battle, that the beaks were not turned towards each other but towards the stone, which they were striking together, carving side by side. Carlo's presence does not interrupt them, does not divert them from their mission, even when he dials the *mairie* and explains the situation. Then, stretching out his arms above the birds of prey, he photographs the memorial stone on which the beaks are clashing and writing:

Having gone in search of myself in the deepest bowels of the unreachable underworld, I had to use the old Celtic weapons, those that move me, that revive the dead or those who thought they were dead. At the end of the crossing, of the great tour of the seas, of the gyres returning endlessly to their point of departure, I can at last come back as they all came back, my companions on the final journey, my brothers of the abyss, of dust. Once again they straddle their lands, completing the cycle of journeys through the volunteers, descendants chosen for superhuman missions, to take these dead ancestors on their backs and lead them to their final grave.

The rage has dissipated, quenched by the brave who continue along the path of oleanders and violets. Guided by the verses of the enchanter poet, they continue to draw lines in the dark skies.

Nothing has gone.